C000193496

What He Really Wants

What He
Really
Wants
Is A Dog

Stories by
Katie Campbell

for Sheilagh
looking forward to the novel
with best wishes

Katie

Lamb Bench
21. 9. 90

Methuen

'Author's Tour' and
'Manhattan, New York City, America, The World',
were first broadcast on 'Morning Story'.

'Famous Blue Raincoat' was commissioned by
BBC English for 'Tales of Today',
and first broadcast on the BBC World Service.

'Bullshit' first appeared in *Slow Dancer*
and 'Author's Tour' in the *Critical Quarterly*,
Manchester University Press.

'The Embankment' by T.E.Hulme is taken
from *The Penguin Book of Imagist Poets*.

The poem in 'Morning'
is taken from *The Psychoed*
by Hughes Mearns.

First published in Great Britain 1989
by Methuen London
81 Fulham Road, London sw3 6rb
Copyright © 1989 Katie Campbell

A CIP catalogue record
for this book is available
from the British Library.

isbn 0 413 62310 6

Printed and bound in Great Britain
by

St Edmundsbury Press,
Bury St Edmunds,Suffolk

For Bruce

Contents

Thirteen
Scenes of Betrayal
In Or About
Key West

I

'Was it hard to get a room?'

'It wasn't bad.'

'There's something I want . . . I want to explain . . .'
She slid along the plastic, her thighs sticking in the heat.
He locked her coat in the trunk and climbed into the driver's
seat. 'I think . . . I want my own room.'

He manoeuvered out of the parking lot and drove for a
few minutes in silence. She was relieved to get out of the
airport. Her friends weren't the sort to visit Miami, but you
could never be sure who you'd meet in an airport.

He took one hand from the steering wheel to adjust the air
conditioning. 'Why don't you wait and see?' he suggested. 'If
you're not feeling amorous we can just cuddle.' She drew in a
breath to protest. 'I've been looking forward to this for a very
long time,' he cut in. 'I would be awfully disappointed if we
don't at least share a room.'

II

They drove down the strip of highway; the land was getting
narrower, the water on both sides was closing in. They passed huge nests on the tops of poles. The poles were holding
up signs saying 'Ted and Ron's Rooms', 'Mama Macamba's
Home Cooked Meals'. The nests were huge and hairy, like
enormous heads on thin, stick necks. The highway was lined
with laundromats, used car lots, discount drug stores. People
live here, she thought to herself. People have real lives here.

He was telling her about the old man beside him in the arrivals lounge: his wife was dying of cancer; he'd gone down ahead to rent them a place; he was afraid she would be too weak but she had insisted; she wanted to die in the sun.

The water was green. The sky was blue. The grass was sparse and looked like plastic, as did the palm trees, bent in the wind, fringing the shore like eyelashes. The sun was dull and hazy in the evening light.

III

They turned off the highway into a parking lot – the Sea Breeze Motor Inn. She wondered if she had packed the right clothes; she had known it would be hot, but she hadn't really believed it.

'I thought we'd save the extra cash for treats,' he said, climbing out of the car, 'after all, we're just sleeping here.' He told her not to hurry. Relax in the car while he checked them in. He returned with the key. Room 214.

IV

'It looks . . . comfortable. I've never seen such wide beds.'

The air conditioning roared. The room was too cold. She switched off the air conditioning. Then she closed the curtains and switched on the lights. He switched them off.

V

'Let's go for a big breakfast,' he said. 'I usually eat a big breakfast.'

'I don't eat breakfast,' she said, 'but I'll sit with you.'

'Let's go to the Holiday Inn down the road. It serves real hash browns. One thing I can't stand is reconstituted potatoes.'

They walked along the highway, past the Quality Inn, the Best Western, the Howard Johnson. She wondered if he had signed in as a single. The chamber maid would know there were two of them when she saw the sheets.

The Holiday Inn had a pool and a landscaped garden. The grass was thicker here than on the roadsides, though it still looked like plastic. The restaurant was silent, muffled by thick, pink carpets. They were given a corner table. She watched a couple through the window: a fat woman, dripping water over her baby's head. A man put down his paper and looked at them adoringly.

'They have good tea if I remember right,' he said, trying to get her attention. 'Darjeeling, I believe.' They didn't. They had ordinary coffee or ordinary tea. Or orange juice, canned. But the hash browns were good. 'I stayed here last year,' he explained. She was staring again at the couple; they were taking turns swinging their baby in the pool.

VI

She let him take her hand. She hated holding hands. He wore shorts and knee socks. 'Dressed like a Miami Jew,' he'd chuckled, lacing up his shoes. He pronounced it with three syllables, the second one being 'Yam'.

She wore a sundress and sandals; her white arms and legs were covered in sunscreen. She looked like a little girl. He looked like a little boy. He could be her paediatrician, but she didn't look scarred enough to have children. He could be her professor but she looked too old to be a student. He could be her accountant, but it was the middle of the week.

The traffic slid along beside them, big cars cruising slowly in the heat. The breeze smelled like a greenhouse or a swimming pool – moist, hot, carrying chlorine. The coconuts weren't ripe, he explained, neither were the bananas. Small green fingers. She never would have noticed them. She never would have guessed they were bananas.

VII

They drove into the centre and parked beside the wharf. He wanted to show her the old town, the eyebrow houses jammed in together with their tiny windows in the rooves.

People slept in those rooms despite the heat. The rooves were tin to stop the sparks from spreading if one house caught on fire. 'Imagine the noise of the rain on those rooves.'

'I'll bet it sounds like calypso,' he said. It sounded like he'd said it before.

Elaborate black ironwork held up the porches, or white gingerbread, elegantly carved: initials, peace signs, voodoo symbols. Walking past the cemetery she saw a rooster on a grave. Last year he'd almost bought one of the eyebrow houses, the 'native' houses. 'Could have got it for eighty grand; fixed it up, would be worth double that today.' He took her past the house. They walked down three lanes before he found the right one. It was fixed up; it was for sale again.

VIII

He took her to dinner on the terrace of the Reach Hotel. The *Queen of Alaska* was docked alongside it. 'From the northernmost point of America,' he said. They'd seen it earlier, a white patch on the ocean. It drew twenty-five foot of water, she could see from the numbers on its hull. They hadn't been back to the motel to change. She would have been more comfortable in Denny's on Duval Street. They were the only ones on the terrace. It was early. People were still swimming. There was no one else to serve so the waiter kept fluttering down to see if they wanted anything. They wanted to be left alone.

She ordered a pineapple daiquiri. The pineapple was canned. He had a rum and Coke. He didn't usually drink; he had it to keep her company.

He wished she'd talk more. He seemed to do all the talking.

He said, 'I hope I'm not talking too much.'

She said, 'Oh no, you're entertaining me.'

He said, 'I wish you'd say more.'

She said, 'I haven't much to say.'

A crowd of kids spilled onto the terrace shrieking, giggling, ordering drinks. She watched the sailors carrying crates up the gangplank, disappearing into the *Queen of Alaska*. He told her the story of his Aunt Pearl and Uncle Len. Pearl nagged

14

at Len until he split her head in two with an axe. They got him off on provocation. Two weeks later he shot himself. He couldn't live without her. Couldn't live with her; couldn't live without her.

IX

They walked to the dock to watch the sun go down. 'This is what everyone does,' he explained. The streets were filled with people strolling down towards the water. The dock was already crowded. Pockets of people surrounded the juggler, the contortionist, the Frenchman dressed as a lion tamer with his trio of trained house cats, the fat woman miming *Wizard of Oz* songs to a scratchy tape, the palm reader, the caricaturist, the graphologist, the tarot reader, the jeweller, the painter, the puppeteer, the one-man band. She could hear a bagpipe playing from the far end of the dock.

They pushed their way between the people. The place smelled of popcorn and patchouli. There was no space left on the edge of the wharf; people were jammed together, hip to hip, legs swinging over the edge. The sun was round and red as an eyeball. Falling fast. Gradually the noise declined, first the one-man band, then the singer; then the noise of the audience as all the acts paused. Only the piper played on.

Suddenly the sun touched the line of the horizon. She almost expected it to sizzle. A third, a half, three quarters sunk: it sent out a fan of golden rays. Then there was only a sliver of sun, gilding the clouds lined up in its path. Then it fell. Still. Applause. Then everybody shuffled off. The acts resumed, the people chattered, beneath it all the piper played.

'Three minutes,' a kid behind them announced.

'What's that?' an old woman queried.

'5:58 to 6:01. Last night it was three minutes fourteen seconds.'

She sat on the dock, dangling her legs above the grey water.

'Edges,' he said. 'I like to be on the edges of things. Here we are, you and me, on the southernmost tip of America. Ninety miles to Cuba. Ocean all the way . . .'

15

Two kids were necking in a boat bobbing a few yards away in the water. She wrapped his arms around her, rocking back and forth, side to side, pitching and yawing as the sky turned from pink to blue, and a strange beam of green spread across the horizon. Eventually even the green disappeared. Their bare legs scraped the concrete, their backs ached, their arms grew numb. They rocked till it was dark. They didn't speak.

X

She was relieved to see the bed had been made. She wondered if the maid would report that there were two of them in the room. The curtain was open and the air conditioning was on. The room was too cold again. She closed the curtain and opened the door to let the room warm up.

He wanted to swim; she didn't. He went off to the pool at the Holiday Inn. She wanted to walk on the beach but she didn't have a key. She couldn't leave the room unlocked because his money was there. She couldn't take it with her in case he thought she'd been snooping. His sponge bag was open on the sink. It was full of little bottles. The pockets of his suitcase bulged with gift shop packages.

Gideon's Bible. A map of Key West. A Guide To Florida And The Keys. A complaint sheet. A shoe shine cloth. There was nothing to read. She lay on the bed. He'd been gone for over an hour. She wondered if he was ringing his wife. She was asleep when he returned.

XI

At the Hemingway House he paid their entrance fee then left her to take the tour alone. He'd been there before, he said; he wanted to read his newspaper. He found a chair under a banyan tree from which he could watch her walking past the windows in the house.

When the tour was over she went round again. She moved slowly through the bedrooms, imagining she was Pauline Hemingway. When she took the verandah round the outside of the second storey she knew he was watching her from the garden. She didn't look down. She knew he was watching her but she wouldn't look down.

XII

He locked her bag into the trunk beside the winter coat then went to settle up. He left her the keys so she could listen to the radio. She couldn't get the key to turn. She opened all the windows and sat in the front seat, waiting.

It was hot. She didn't want to get a tan. She spread sunscreen over her arms and legs and face. And waited. She pulled off her sandals and rubbed her feet with sunscreen. She wished she'd remembered to use cream on her feet before she'd come. They were scratchy and hard. She noticed a collar of hairs around her ankle. She'd shaved her legs in a hurry. He was bound to have seen the hairs. And her toenails were dirty beneath the chipped paint. She wondered if he'd noticed that as well, last night or the night before. She didn't care.

She looked at herself in the mirror. Her eyes were red. Hot and tired. They seemed to have more wrinkles than when she arrived. Sun dries skin. She rubbed some cream into the lines. She waited. Perhaps there was some trouble with his credit card. She had some cash, but he wouldn't take it anyway. Her eyes were stinging. As she rubbed them he came up behind her. She jumped. He kissed her forehead.

'I know. I hate to leave you too.'

'No, I wasn't crying . . .' She let it drop.

He wrapped his arms around her. His back was wet with sweat. Her arms were sticky with sunscreen. 'We'd better hit the road,' he said. 'The traffic might be heavy round Miyami.'

XIII

He wanted to stop for one more kiss. She was afraid she'd miss the flight. They didn't stop; they drove. The Gulf of Mexico on one side, the Atlantic on the other; they drove the thin highway dividing the waters.

17

They arrived at the airport an hour before her departure. He insisted on waiting. He found her a seat then telephoned his folks. They were expecting him. He would be late.

She watched his reflection in the glass, pretending to look at the planes taking off. The first phone he tried wasn't working. He moved on to the next. His head moved, animated; probably his mother, she decided. Then a gesture of surprise. Then a new conversation. Then he hung up.

'Everything okay?' she asked.

'My sister and her kids are there.'

'Did you know they were coming?'

'They were touring the south; decided to drop in on Grandma. She says they just came up from Key West.'

'Do you think they saw us?'

He shook his head. 'She said if she'd known I was there she'd have looked me up.'

Her flight was called. A passenger was paged. She froze. 'My husband; that's my husband's name.' She peered round a pillar at the queue.

'Funny,' he said, 'it never occurred to me to ask your married name. I assumed you used his.'

'Of course it couldn't be him,' she muttered, 'he's in Oregon all week. There's no way he could be in Miami.'

He insisted on carrying her bag.

'Thanks,' she said, when they got to the gate. 'It-was . . . Well. Thanks.'

He slipped something into her pocket. A key ring with a little gold key with 'A key to my heart from the Florida Keys' written across it. 'A little thing to remember this time.'

'I won't need to remember it,' she smiled, 'but thanks anyway.' She'd have to leave it on the plane; she couldn't explain a Florida key ring. She shuffled forward. 'You'd better get back on the road,' she said. He nodded, and blew her one last kiss.

When she looked back he was striding quickly towards the exit. When he turned to wave one last goodbye, she had already disappeared.

*Dirty
Linen*

It would have been unfair to lay blame – not that anybody did. Everybody assumed it was Virgil, but Cabbage was really just as confused. They were, you could say, the products of a broken home.

Cabbage – who was named for the darting Cabbage White butterflies she resembled as a kitten – Cabbage was suspicious of people. Steve got her from a pet shop to replace Pushkin who disappeared one time when Sal was away and he was in charge. Cabbage enjoyed human company but hated being patted, especially by men. Steve joked that she and Sal were two of a kind.

Secretly Steve was put out because Cabbage ignored him. Worse than that, she would sit on the lid of the loo while he took his bath and as soon as the water drained away she'd slide inside and roll on the hot, smooth porcelain, emitting squeals of delight. Steve found this rather distasteful, but he never stopped her; he hoped to develop a rapport with the cat.

Virgil on the other hand – he was named after a rotund composer – Virgil adored people. Indeed he was so trusting that he inspired people to abuse him. Steve particularly enjoyed hanging him upsidedown by his back legs, an exercise which transported Virgil into throes of ecstasy. Virgil's only problem was that he drooled – everywhere, always, and completely without shame. Sal decided that he had been taken away from his mother too young; this would also explain his unhealthy trust in human beings, most notably in Steve.

The trouble began when Sal and Steve decided to move. They bought a new house, a dream house, a stage set for the rest of their lives.

'This will be the foundation for that leap from cats to kids . . .' Steve joked; a joke which Sal rose above because it touched on a sore point between them.

'Forget it, Steve, you can't even remember to buy the cat food!'

'That doesn't mean I don't love the cats.'

'It means you don't Take Responsibility for them.'

'When it's kids I will Take Responsibility.'

'For Christ's sake, Steve; you retch when you're faced with a bit of catshit – you're not going to cope with crappy nappies.' And so it went . . .

The old house was duly abandoned, but although the builders promised that the new house would be ready, when the time came to move, the bedroom was the only space that was habitable. Steve was not amused at the prospect of sharing his bedroom with Sal, plus the cats plus their food and litter tray. 'Right, sir; got the picture. I'll tell the gov'nor how you feel.' The gov'nor was never on site, having several other jobs to oversee, so Steve was dependent on the chippie or the brickie or the sparkie to relay his displeasure.

The first night, Steve muttered blackly: 'Why did we bother to move anyway?'

From the opposite side of the bed Sal replied sweetly, 'Because you wanted to live in Kensington, dear.'

As for the cats, they found it all a great adventure. The bedroom was in fact a suite, with a bathroom on one side and a dressing room on the other, so although they weren't used to being confined, they did have some space in which to race about. And race about they did.

On the second night the cats calmed down, but the bedroom roof leaked. Despite Sal's protestations, Steve spent the night chasing the drips with the toothbrush mug. The third night passed uneventfully except that Steve and Sal were both exhausted from their lack of sleep. The fourth night it rained again and the pitch that the builders put on the roof as a temporary repair came dripping through in sticky globs. The fifth night was marred by the doorbell ringing at dawn when the brickie, back from Ireland, arrived on site and found that the key was not in its usual place.

After a fortnight, Sal feigned flu and took a day off work to put some order into the room. The window ledge was lined with cartons of moulding milk, and the floor was gritty with kitty litter and crushed catfood. She bought a broom and rubbish bags and an ironing board, and spent the afternoon ironing sheets. At five she moved from the bedroom to the bathroom, and while scrubbing the mirror over the sink, she noticed four grey hairs stemming from the top of her head. At seven Steve rang to say he would be late again tonight. At nine she tried to brush the cats who had no intention of submitting to such indignity. At eleven she folded the ironed sheets and placed them in the laundry basket, in the dressing room. Then she wandered vaguely around the room, wondering what to do next.

At midnight Steve returned. He didn't notice that Sal had swept the floor and washed the clothes and replaced the foetid milk. He kicked off his shoes, dropped on the freshly-made bed and, grabbing the remote control handset, switched on the television and flicked quickly through the channels.

Sal retreated to the bathroom, showered, shampooed, shaved her legs, and dried herself with the hand towel she had saved from the storage van. Then she rubbed cream all over her body, paying particular attention to elbows and knees as they advised in the magazines of her youth. Then she painted her toenails (red) and her fingernails (clear), sprayed perfume in her damp hair and emerged into the bedroom where Steve was snoring through the riot reports on the late night news.

Sal turned off the television and slid in beside him. 'Darling,' she cooed. He woke with a start. 'I've decided: I want us to have a child . . .'

'What?' he scowled, struggling to comprehend the sudden silence.

'Now, with the new house and all; if we conceive this week it will arrive in time for the autumn recruits to cover my maternity leave . . .'

Steve jumped off the bed. 'No,' he muttered.

'What?'

'I don't want a child . . .'

'What do you mean!'

'It's all changed.'

'But, Steve. It's *you* who always wanted a baby!'

'No. Not now. The time isn't right . . .'

'But it was *you* . . .'

'I have to get away.'

'We've just got back from holiday.'

'Apart. Alone.'

'I don't understand.'

'Sal, I want a separation.'

He explained he'd been thinking about this for several weeks – since they'd sold the old house in fact; he'd just been waiting for the right time to tell her. She was convinced it was just that the new house was in such a mess. He assured her it was the relationship not the mess that he was leaving. She pleaded. He was unmoved. She eventually cried herself to sleep. He spent the night on top of the blankets. The cats slept in the corner.

The following morning Steve left. Sal remained in bed that day, explaining to the office that her twenty-four hour flu had extended itself. The builders, assuming she was sick, were as unobtrusive as builders can be. The cats raced around spitting and hissing.

Sal slept and cried and turned on the television. Then she slept and cried some more. As dusk was falling she noticed the basket of laundry through the dressing room door; she noticed something dark on the smooth, white sheet. She stared for several minutes before her curiosity overcame her inertia and she climbed out of the bed to investigate.

What she had seen was catshit, a small pyramid of catshit on the smooth, white pane of the freshly-ironed sheet. She stared at it for a few minutes, then returned to her bed.

The next morning Sal pulled herself together and went into work. The boss, assuming her swollen eyes were the results of a still-raging flu, insisted that she go back to bed. On the way home she bought a bottle of bleach and a roll of paper towels to clean up the catshit. On entering the house, however, she lost all incentive and climbed into bed.

Over the next few days Sal got up, dressed, undressed, ate cereal from her used coffee cup, read the newspaper cover to cover – including, especially, the television listings and the personal columns; then she made newspaper balls for the cats who generally ignored them. After listening to the midday news she'd follow the afternoon soaps on TV. Several times a day she would glance inside the laundry basket.

On the first day the catshit transmuted from damp to clay-like. On the second day it had a thin outer cover, like the skin on a scab. By the third day it was crisp. By the fourth it was almost hard. By the fifth day it was dry as a bone.

While Cabbage simply rose above the excrement, Virgil was disturbed. At first he would accompany Sal and examine the pyramid, tentatively, as though trying to ascertain what it was and to whom it belonged. Then he began to avoid it. Eventually he steered clear of the dressing room altogether.

After a week Sal went back to work. The builders made an effort to finish the job. Pete, the painter, explained one evening over a cup of tea: 'It often happens, love; don't worry, he'll be back, soon as we're all outa here. Jealous, i'n't he: eight of us tippin' up here each morning; and the noise and all. Don't you worry, he'll come back.'

But she knew he wouldn't.

By now the cats were running freely through the premises so Sal relegated their litter tray to the dustbin along with various important and unimportant papers Steve had left behind. The builders moved into the final stages, laying carpets, installing light switches. And throughout it all the catshit remained.

Steve had to return to the house several times during the negotiations. On his first visit he noticed the catshit. On each succeeding visit he passed through the dressing room, and each time he thought that the catshit seemed to grow, imperceptibly, smaller. He never mentioned this to Sal – neither the catshit nor its diminution. And she, if she noticed either, never mentioned them to him.

When the decorating was complete and the separation was secured, the estate agent came to make an appraisal. As he made his slow, relentless progress through the rooms, he paused a moment in front of the laundry basket. Then he moved rapidly on, extolling, as he went, the virtues of industrial cleaners. Then the evaluator came. He passed so quickly through the room that he barely noticed the laundry basket, and certainly didn't investigate. Then the surveyor came and didn't even bother to enter the dressing room.

And by the time the first prospective buyer came to examine the house, the catshit had diminished to a mere shadow, a flick of dust, like a whisper of ash brushed carelessly from an unguarded cigarette.

*Chorus
from
the Rock*

DARLENE:

I should have seen it coming. I should have said No. I should have screamed Are you Crazy No Fucking Way! I should have stopped it all before it started.

When it was all over they said they thought I realized. They thought I understood. They thought we all agreed. She said she thought he'd told me. He said he thought I knew I mean what the hell did you think I was doing you were always busy and you suggested You Suggested I take her out. I mean what the hell were you saying to me?

She was alone, going through rough times. She had bad luck with men. They either left or beat up on her. She was lovely. She was my best friend. And each man who came along she thought he was the one.

I was pregnant. Busy with the new house. So I said yes I did suggest he go up occasionally. And he couldn't afford to stay in a hotel or anything and she had the sofabed so it was only natural. I mean, I'd slept on it myself. When we were moving and all and the sheets and things had been sent on ahead. And when he was away on the road I'd move over to her place because it was fun for us together. Fun. I never had sisters but I'm sure that's what it's like. The sofa was old. Rusty hinges. So we had to wrestle to get the double bed out. That always ended with a tumble and a giggle. Then we'd lie there for hours drinking whisky sours, watching late night films and talking. Talking. She wanted a baby. That's all she ever wanted was a baby she could love. And we'd tell each other about the men we'd had before.

29

And sometimes we talked so late she'd fall asleep in the bed with me.

Her bedroom has a single bed. They must have slept in the lounge. Pulled out the old sofa-bed like we did. She and me. He wouldn't let her help. He'd have done it. She'd have watched. I wonder if they laughed the way we did. She and me.

He promised not to see her. Ever again. He doesn't. I know he doesn't. He never leaves us now. Me and the baby. He loves the baby. He feels real bad about it all. I miss her now. I hear she's found an other man. Who beats her up.

PAT:

I rang him up and told him about the fight, the broken window. He was shocked. No, surprised. Maybe angry. He didn't realize we bothered to fight each other any more. He said he couldn't see me for a few days. It was a week before he came round. They came round.

It was a party. Saturday night. He didn't look at me all evening. I kept trying to catch his eye. He was talking to somebody, somebody else, when I came into the room. I led him away pretending I needed someone to open the wine. We didn't speak. I led him to the bedroom. Into the room. To the window. He stood at the end of the bed. Stared. The pane was shattered. Jagged. Edges sticking up. Hanging down. He didn't speak. The light was off. We could see from the street. The moon was in water that night. I wanted to tell him. I wanted to show him. I lowered my hand on a piece of the glass. He didn't speak. I watched his eyes his eyes on my hand my palm, a piece of the glass pierced my palm. It bled on the sheet the mattress beneath. Even the mattress beneath it was stained.

He watched the blood. I watched him watching. Quietly. He turned. Downstairs to the party to his wife he got his wife he got her took her hand and left. I haven't spoken to him since.

MANDY:

He rang the night before he left. He said he'd be too busy to write but he'd ring. It's been three weeks and nothing yet. I've written to him so there'll be something from me when he gets back. I thought he would have rung by now. I still have his voice on the answerphone. Someone spoke over most of it, so there's only a few words left. But I listen to it sometimes last thing before bed. Almost every night.

I still dream about him sometimes. When we're making love. I imagine it's him. His face above me. His smile which I can't see but I know is there. Smiling at some private joke. Absorbed in him. And me. And when we finish and roll over and he curls himself beside me. Thinner, smaller. Somehow less encompassing. I am always shocked to realize. The man I was making love to is not him at all.

I still dream about him. I see him. But there's something wrong. He's dyed his hair. Or his eyes are funny. And I'm following him and he's way ahead of me and I'm trying to get his attention and I can't bring myself to shout. But finally I do. Shout. And finally he does turn around. And he smiles at me sadly. And turns and walks away. And I stand there staring as he goes. And once again I'm left alone.

LIZ:

I still dream about him all the time. I dream of smashing his head against the pavement till it splits. Soft and mushy. Full of dirt and bits of brick. And I dream of taking a knife and slicing his face. His cheeks. His smooth baby cheeks till they bleed till there's nothing left except blood.

And I dream of kicking him in the groin. In the balls, in the nuts, in the goolies. Kicking him in the soft bits with a pair of big construction boots. Steel toes and lead soles and when he doubles over I'll smash him over the head with a fist.

He'll wriggle in the dirt and I'll kick him till he isn't even squirming. And the quieter he is the more I will despise him and I'll kick kick kick until there's nothing there but stick and sick and slime and I'll punch it with my fist and it will hit right through to pavement and in the pain and with an aching fist I'll straighten up. And spit. Then I'll walk away.

JILL:

Fuck it, who wants 'em, they say it's like shitting a watermelon, like stretching your lower lip over your head, like hell; they say it's like dying, they say it's like some sort of ecstasy, some sort of ecstatic cosmic orgasm. Of course the ones who say it's wonderful are the ones who've never done it, never will, it's always the men who say it's wonderful.

It's like being a beetle. Like being a moon, a balloon, a gigantic roach, like shitting a tree, giving birth to the earth, as round and smooth and fat as a fat-cheeked Buddah.

All that sick and stick and stink and slime and smelling like sponge all the time. And the breasts. Big breasts. Big bovine breasts. So vulnerable, big bellies and breasts. Women with big bellies and breasts.

RUTH:

We stood there. In front of them all. Him beside me, nervous. I could smell it. I was not. For once in my life I wasn't nervous, I was . . . confident. From the moment I woke up that day I knew what to do. I knew what to say. I said it. In that place full of people. I said the words. Careful. Confidently. Loud. I do, I said. I said the words. I heard them echo. I was satisfied.

When his turn came he faltered. Trembled. I wouldn't have thought it. He's always been so confident, assured, so self-assured, so full of himself. He said his lines and he looked at me and even after the organ started I could hear my last line echoing: I do.

LINDA:

It's not that I fancied him. Not that at all. I just hated the idea of hitting middle age and not having had an affair. An Extra Marital Affair. An Extra. Something more. More than this this this. This Life. When I get to Saint Peter, or is it Saint Paul? When I get to those gates I want to have More. Adultery. I want to have Adulteress beside my name.

So I rang him. No. He rang me. He rang me about once a month. And we'd meet. I'd say I was going for a night with the girls and we'd meet in the pub. It's a wine bar now, but it's really just a pub that serves salad. I always hoped one of the girls from work would see us there but they never did, or if they did they didn't say.

Anyway, my husband said he was going away on business. Didn't give me any warning, just up and says he has to go. He knows I hate being on my own but he says he can't help it and what do I expect him to do quit the job and then what will we live on so up he gets and goes. Just like that.

So he rings. I wouldn't have planned it but as it happened I said why not and I always say I can't stay late but this time I say why not make it dinner? Well that stumps him 'cause he's married too. He always rings her when we're leaving so she can put the dinner on. I wonder if she knows who he's been with, but I won't ask and he won't say. It's a thing we do. Neither asks about the other's marriage. As if it wasn't there. But of course it is, it's all we really care about.

We always meet at half past six. He's there first, drinking beer, no boss to wait for, one last letter, call, one cup to wash up. So he's there in the usual place only this time he has a glass of white wine and one for me, a drink-before-dinner, he says, and he's booked us a table for seven at the Frenchie down the road. So we drink it and another and then on to dinner and this and that. He comes back with me in a cab. I usually take the bus but when we get there, well, he's never been inside the place but seems to know the street and suddenly I realize, I bet he's driven past it. I bet he's looked up the address and driven past to see the place I live now.

33

So anyway he comes in for a drink. And I say shouldn't you ring your wife, because it's late now, near midnight, and usually he's home by eight. But he says no sweat. And he looks around and I see him thinking, Oh, so this is why she left me. But it isn't. But he'll never understand. But it doesn't matter anyway since we don't even like each other now. I don't think we ever did.

Anyway, and so it goes and we end up of course in the bedroom – he asks for a tour of the place and so we end up, of course, in the bed. And we do it. Of course. And it's just like it was two, no three, four years ago. He does it like he always did. Nothing's changed. Hasn't learned new tricks from her. For her. For me. Then I say, You know it's two in the morning, shouldn't you phone her or something? He says no sweat. I told her it was business. Wasn't she upset? I say. So what does she expect me to do, quit the job? I told her I'd be away one night maybe two. So we spent that night and the next together till my husband got back.

Well it's her problem, isn't it, it isn't mine – I got rid of him years ago. If he wants to spend his nights with me . . . It was nice after all that time. It was easy. It was nothing. It was . . . Adultery. At least thank God I don't have to face middle age without having had an affair.

DIANA:

Shit, I wish it was a mistress. A mistress I could deal with. At least I'd have the moral advantage then. And sympathy.

I know they call me a bitch and a shrew. A social professional liability. And all those little secretaries with co-ordinated stockings who cream themselves to bring him coffee thinking they could make him happy.

Fuck it. They can have him. Wish they would. Wish they'd take him off my hands. They won't though, won't be able to. You see, he is a coward. He hasn't the guts, the imagination, to take on a mistress. And the thing is, even if he did, even if I did leave him, even if I found a reason, he wouldn't care. He would be happy just the same. Successful.

Despite me. To spite me. And that I couldn't bear. Not the spite – the success.

The only release for me is if he dies. I dream about it. Every day. I dream about him dying. I dream the death. Each detail. Down to the dress I'll wear.

EVELYN:

I woke up feeling awful. Not morning sickness. Pains. Then the bleeding began. I felt all sick and sticky. He called the doctor; she said get to bed. When she arrived the blood was all over. She said it was a miscarriage. Nothing to do but sit on the can and get rid of it. She said she'd had five herself – miscarriages. Just sit on the can, she said. Push it out.

I sat on the can. And pushed. It wouldn't come. I could feel it hanging there and I screamed and it wouldn't let go. It was hanging out of me. Half in half out. It wouldn't let go. And I screamed for him to pull it out and he wouldn't and I screamed. They gave me an injection. The blood was everywhere. They used newspaper to mop it up. Then I slept.

I still don't know if they pulled or if it just came. Or if it fell out in the can when I was screaming. I still feel it hanging inside me sometimes. The doctor said that she'd had five – miscarriages. Maybe it's something they say. I wonder how many are flushed away. Sometimes I can't help thinking about it. All the babies. Not babies, miscarriages. Flushed away, in the sewers. And I think of the crocodiles in New York City.

SUE:

He's afraid of me. That's it, I'm sure. At first it was he pursuing me. That night when he asked about past lovers, when he asked if there was anyone now. I was thinking as he spoke: these are the questions lovers ask each other. The very fact we're talking about sex implies an intimacy.

All those times. In public. When he asked everybody how they kissed; he looked at me while he asked each of them – you could see it was *me* he wanted to know about.

35

And that other time, when I asked where you had gone and he leaned over. I thought he was going to whisper to me. I thought he was going to whisper you had gone to the loo. But he didn't whisper, he kissed my cheek. I'm sure he kissed my cheek. Then he sat back as though nothing had happened. And all through the second act my cheek screamed, He Kissed Me. He Kissed Me. I kept looking at him down the row. And his eyes were on the orchestra. By the end of the concert I didn't know whether he really had. Kissed me.

And then the other time when we were all queueing for tickets and he came up behind me in front of everyone. He put his arms around me and said, quite quietly but it wasn't a whisper, I love you. I couldn't believe it. So calmly. As though it was no big deal. And I knew that in an hour I wouldn't know if it had really happened, so I said, slowly, deliberately, I love you too. And I said to myself as I said it, This is real. The words: I love you too. I said those words. I formed them. Felt them. Savoured them as I forced them through my mouth and off my lips. And I said to myself. This. At least. At last. Is real. But already I'm wondering if it was.

VERITY:

When I turned over he was sitting there on the bed. His pants and socks and shirt and tie on. Staring at me. He should have left twenty minutes ago. So I asked what was wrong. I should have put my arms around him. But I didn't.

He wanted kids so badly. Sure he wanted them. He would, wouldn't he? All he's sacrificing is a few hundred sperm. He sacrifices that every night. Well, twice a week. Regular as clockwork. Not twenty years.

We've been at each other's throats for so long now, he spends all his time at work or working at home late at night if he isn't watching television.

Working at home. Working at home. Having a bath. Washing the dishes. Packing to go to a conference. Unpacking. Going for a job, a swim, a game of squash, a dinner with friends, a drink, a meal, a cup of tea. Reading a book, reading a paper, reading a report, reading a Very Important Report. These are the ways we avoid making love.

So I turned to him one night when I was in bed and he was doing something, fixing his stamps or cutting his hair or toenails or something, I turned to him and I said, Shall we have a baby? . . . What he really wants is a dog.

ANN:

It was no big deal. I rang him in New York. Explained what had happened. He could have said Get Lost. I could have put the thing in wrong. I could have forgotten it altogether. I hate the damn thing anyway, smelling of rubber and slime. Not that he'd have noticed. He never asked about it once, he just assumed. He didn't use anything himself. Catch him wearing one of those things – No Fucking Way! Anyway I told him I'd found a place, in the country – an old stately home. A hundred and thirty quid, about two hundred bucks, all very civilized, you paid in cash. He sent a money order for the exact amount: one hundred and thirty pounds sterling. Nothing for transport. And I had to buy a nightgown.

I got off the train at this country platform; a cab was waiting to take me to the place. Doctors and nurses dressed in white and everyone cool and polite. The nurses were mostly black. One or two Indians. The doctors were men: young men, easy money. The older ones hate doing it.

The place was full of women in those silly little hospital things that barely cover your pubes. I didn't have supper. The next morning they wheeled me in – it took about twenty minutes, I suppose. It's hard to tell.

In the room next to mine a woman screamed for hours. They wheeled me into the lounge because they needed my bed for the afternoon lot. They do three lots a day on weekends and two on weekdays. Housewives, I suppose. There were twenty in our group. Women like me, women with jobs. A few younger girls of sixteen or seventeen, in from the provinces. They described their blokes; the stories they'd made up to get to the clinic. Made a joke of it. Said they were going on a shopping trip. A nurse passed out biscuits and tea. Next to the sugar bowl was a pile of pamphlets about contraception. Nobody touched them. After an hour or so they said I could go. So I went.

SHARON:

The old fucker was all sweetness and light. I should have known. Anything I can do just give me a ring. Anytime. Just try it. We went out one night. He kept ringing me so I said, Why not? I mean, he was my landlord, I needed the place; it's tough to find places to live in this city. I couldn't say No, I mean, I tried to make it clear but when he started I couldn't stop him. I didn't want to make him mad, I mean, places are hard to come by. And I figured what the hell, I won't go out with him again. Think of it as a key deposit or a month's rent in advance. He said, Let's celebrate, then he drank. Whisky. Stinking whisky. Wouldn't stop. So it happened. And what do you think? Well, it could have been worse. I mean, I could have got pregnant. He gave me herpes. I mean, I didn't have it before and I did have it after.

I rang him. He denied it then hung up. So I told the doctor anyway. I mean I had to tell him. I mean, the doctor had to know. Then it begins – I get a letter saying they want me out, they need the space. Then he gets the builders in. Beer bellies leering round the place, leaving their tools for people to trip on. I went down to the city council; they say it's illegal, but do they do a thing? Not a jot, not a sausage, not on your life. I even get hold of my congressman. We'll get this guy. All smiles and sympathetic nods. Too sympathetic. Next thing I hear he's holidaying in Sicily. I mean, who the hell knows where Sicily is!

And now with winter coming on and no hot water, it's no joke. Then suddenly I see these things. Beetles. Crawling round the can. I remember how I said it that first time, that night we spent together and the time before when I signed the lease, The one thing I can't stand is bugs. Roaches – I can't stand a place with roaches. He made a joke. He heard me. He remembered. So I set down powder but it's no good, they're all over, in the toilet, the lounge. You open a drawer – two, three, five of them shuffle off, like old men. It got so they wouldn't even run – you open the biscuit tin, they're there. Staring at you. You pour out the cereal, you find 'em crawling round in the bowl. It got so bad that they were hanging around in the tampax box. That was the end. When I had to keep the tampax in the fridge, that was the end.

I went to see about buying a gun. For hunting, I said. They didn't believe me. I'll bet you're a vegetarian, the man behind the counter says. His friend spits tobacco juice over my shoe, all green and slimy. Chewed. Sorry, sweetheart, ain't got nothin' in your size. So I bought a butcher's knife and went round to see him. But he'd gone, two months ago. Said they'd never heard of him – no forwarding address. So I left. Just as he meant me to do. I couldn't take anymore. So I left. Just like he wanted.

LOUISE:

Well, what would *you* think? We were sitting there in this fancy restaurant, bottle of champagne between us, he insists he's paying. What are we celebrating? I ask. Nothing, he says. Nothing, us, your marriage, my marriage, tell me about your life. Where do you begin, after all these years? He knew how it was, through friends. He said, and marriage? How does it suit? He knew and he knew I knew he knew, so I shrugged. No point in lying . . . unnecessarily.

So we eat and drink and he tells me about this affair he's having. I thought he of all people would be true. Just think – it could be me, I thought. It could be me he's cheating on. I said it. He says, Maybe if it was you I wouldn't be cheating. I let that one go. So we talk about love and fidelity. He said he thinks you only have one passion in your life. And his is me. I. Me. I was his Great Passion. He and his wife get on, he says, so he'll stay with her. But he'll always have affairs, he says. So we drink some more and the restaurant's closing for the afternoon so we go to this club.

He asks me why I haven't had affairs. I say the right person, right place, haven't happened at the right time. He teases me. Drives me home. Insists. In his BMW. It was a Toyota in my day. I ask if he'd like to come in. I'm showing him round. We get to the bedroom, he comes in to the room. He sits on the bed, my bed, beside me, strokes my legs, arms. I say, Shall we do it? For old times. He strokes me. Let's do it, I say.

He stops. Looks into my face. My eyes. With such. He says – with such a look of triumph, venom, very softly, he says – No. Then he walks down the stairs and out of the house. Not a word. He doesn't even turn around. Bastard. Bloody bastard. I'll bet he had it planned for months.

EVE:

And you think, Oh Christ, there are people out there dying. Really Dying. Horrible Terrible Miserable Deaths. Why am I wittering on about this. But the point is. This is. This is my life.

They say you get the face you deserve at forty. Well I ask you, Do I deserve this face?

So I got my bags and left.

So he got his bags and left.

So he just got up and left.

I dream about him all the time.

Very softly he said No.

Then he walked away.

I miss him. Yes, I do.

And I screamed and screamed.

This at least is real.

But of course already I'm wondering if it is.

This. At least. At last. Is real.

(I still have his voice on the answerphone.)

Delphi

'Grapes are my favourite fruit,' Baby said, 'they're so ordered, so . . . domestic – all those sweet little neat little spheres of juice.'

Ann remembered the grapes at lunch: tiny tendrils hanging like obsolete organs from the twisted stems.'Hmm,' she nodded; she couldn't be bothered to disagree.

'My God it's hot,' David sighed loudly and rolled his eyes. Ann glared at him. 'My God it's hot.' He squirmed, kicking Baby's seat in front of him. 'Baby' wasn't her real name, and she certainly wasn't a baby; she was the new girlfriend of David's oldest friend Christopher. David never liked Christopher's women. Neither did Ann, though she did regret having coined the nickname 'Baby'; it gave a focus to David's contempt for the girl. No; woman. Baby was at least as old as Ann, although unencumbered by children. It was her coyness which irritated Ann; and the way she dressed like a fashion model, rather than the shop clerk she was. Baby was a last minute addition to the trip. Still, Ann thought, her presence was a small price to pay for a week with Christopher.

Ann watched Baby run her painted oval finger round her painted oval lips. Her lips were her most prominent feature: tight and lined like an anus, pursed in a perfect O. Ann longed to stick a fist through those lips to see how far it would penetrate. She didn't dislike Baby; she didn't feel much about her one way or the other. Christopher turned from the driver's seat and kissed Baby's cheek.

'Kindly concentrate on the road,' David scowled, 'we've probably already missed the turn.' He grabbed the map from Baby's lap. Baby reapplied her lipstick and began to hum. Ann

43

wondered if the holiday was going to work. A week with just the three of them had seemed like a such good idea. Now with Baby there it might be a mistake.

The farmhouse was smaller than it looked in the brochure. The pool was unheated. The bedrooms were side by side. 'You could clock a fart through these walls,' David muttered, dumping his luggage. Christopher offered them the double bed, but David demurred: 'After seven years of marriage we can stand a week apart.' Ann wished he hadn't said it.

Minutes later Baby's squeals wafted through the wall, followed by Christopher's 'Shhh,' then silence. Then a giggle. David groaned and wrapped the pillow round his head.

Ann changed her T-shirt and went to explore. Beside the front door was a fireplace with a grill across the top. The grass was rough with weeds and herbs. A rosemary bush grew by the road and beyond it a vineyard sloped down the hill to a large, stone house. The agent had offered them the bigger house as well, but Ann wanted to be as close to Christopher as possible. Besides, as she explained to the others, the hilltop would be cooler.

When Christopher emerged it was dark. David was poking at dead leaves in the swimming pool. Ann was grilling chops. 'Oh that smell!' he exclaimed, 'what's that smell?'

'Rosemary,' Ann said, rubbing a sprig of it over the meat. 'There's rosemary, that's for remembrance.'

'Hamlet,' David shouted.

'Ophelia,' Ann corrected him.

'*Touché,*' Christopher whispered, wrapping his arms around Ann's waist. 'What do you mean by this, David – letting your wife slave over the dinner. She's supposed to be on holiday.' Ann paused a moment before unlacing his arms to rescue a flaming chop.

'Ambrosia; sheer ambrosia.' Christopher picked a crispy bit from the side of the grill then offered his fingers for her to lick.

44

'It's too robust for ambrosia,' Ann teased, 'this is food for Satyrs, not for gods.' At that moment Baby called for Christopher to help her in the bedroom.

'A good swift kick; that's what she needs,' David grumbled ten minutes later. Suddenly Baby appeared, swathed in yellow chiffon. 'Ah. The late Madame Butterfly.'

'David,' Ann warned.

'Oh sorry,' Baby purred. 'Am I late? You should have begun; I don't even eat meat anyway.'

You wouldn't, Ann thought.

After supper Christopher washed up, because Baby had her dress on, and Ann had made the meal, and there was never any question of David doing domestic chores. Meanwhile Baby described the last three episodes of 'Dallas'. When Ann suggested a walk, Christopher jumped at the idea. David went to bed with his book. Baby lit another cigarette and waved them on.

As they set off down the gravel road Ann slipped her hand into Christopher's pocket. It was one of those nights when the stars are so bright and the earth so dark and the sky between them seems eternal.

'Oh God, make small the old star-eaten blanket of a sky/that I might fold it round me and in comfort lie . . .' Ann only quoted poetry when she was slightly drunk or supremely content; tonight she was both.

'Nice. Is it yours?' Christopher asked.

'Wish it was,' she shook her head. 'That's only the end bit. I memorized it years ago; I've forgotten the rest . . . Old age.'

He smiled beside her. 'You're younger than me.'

'Younger in years . . .' she sighed.

'Oh dear,' he replied, 'this sounds serious.'

Ann often wondered how such a nice person could be friends with someone as selfish as David. 'What's the trouble?' Christopher asked. 'Come on, tell Uncle Chris.'

'Oh, Chris . . . I suddenly feel . . . I feel . . .'

45

'Yes . . .' he murmured, suddenly realizing that she was, indeed, serious.

'I feel I have no choices left.' She wished she hadn't said it; it sounded melodramatic. She tried to giggle but it came out a grunt. Oh God, she thought as they walked on in silence.

Suddenly Christopher stopped. 'Choices, what are choices?' he said. 'You make them, then they're gone. Ann,' he said, 'I want to marry. I'm sick of being alone. I want that commitment.' She nodded in the dark. The crickets sang; the air was soft, smelling of embers and wild thyme. 'I know things aren't going well with you and David right now, but I believe, I really do believe marriage can work.'

'Yes, I do too,' she replied.

'I'm going to ask her to marry me.'

'What? Who? Oh . . . Yes. Yes. Of course. I see.' Ann was seized with an image of Baby as a butterfly sizzling in the fire.

'I'm thrilled you like her,' Christopher said. 'I knew you would. Listening to you two in the car . . . I knew it would be alright if you liked her.'

Ann saw Baby flailing in the swimming pool, drowning in her drapery, smothered by a scarf of night as she languished in her chaise. The crickets' chorus suddenly seemed a screech – a cawing, mocking screech in the dead, dry grass, in the thick, black night.

The lights were off when they got back; David's low snores alternated with Baby's throaty breaths. Christopher kissed Ann on the lips and slipped into his room. She paused a moment before opening her door. Perhaps it was her imagination – the smell of mouldy clothes; perhaps David didn't really smell. She wondered if Christopher had a smell. She was pleased to have a bed to herself, except that occasionally, on holiday, she and David overcame their irritation, or fatigue, long enough to make love again.

Ann undressed to the sound of low moans mounting to a muffled squeal. As she climbed into her bed David groaned.

'Is that you?' He flicked on the light. 'That woman. I can't bear her.' Somewhere she was relieved that he hadn't fallen for the flowing clothes.

'You'll have to like her or lump her,' Ann replied.

'It isn't serious? It can't be serious! He can't be serious about her! Is he?' David persisted. 'Christ, if he is, the man has gone mad.'

'Well,' Ann sighed, 'if nothing else, at least in this we are united.'

'And in the boys, and the cars, and the cats, and the cottage, and . . .' David rattled off the list like an injunction. She looked at him. He smiled. Surprised, she smiled back. He leaned from his bed and kissed her, then flicked off the light.

Ann lay in the dark.

'Ann?' David spoke a few minutes later. 'Ann, come here.' She shuddered at the cold bite of the stone floor. 'Ann,' he said, 'I can't take that woman. If Christopher wants to hang around with air-heads that's his business. I can't spent the next six days cooped up in this sardine tin with that woman.'

'It isn't long, six days,' she said. 'We'll take the car tomorrow and go off on our own.'

'No,' he replied, 'I have so little holiday time, I won't have it poisoned by that woman. I'm going home.'

'David, you can't do that! What about Christopher! What about me? It's my holiday too.'

'You stay here. I'll tell them tomorrow; I'll say I've remembered something – an unfinished case. I'm sorry, Ann. I'll take another week next month. We can go off by ourselves. We can take the boys along.'

Ann loved the boys, but she also loved getting away from them. 'I'm sorry, darling. Really.' That was that. She stepped back to her own bed. Next door it was quiet.

In the morning David left amid much sympathy and regret. Baby suggested he telephone his secretary to deal with the problem, Ann offered to come home with him, Christopher volunteered to drive him to the airport. In the end he took

47

the bus. When he sorted himself out in London he would ring them with his plans.

After lunch Baby went inside for a nap. Ann settled beside the pool. Christopher hovered over her, blocking her sun with his shadow. Finally he spoke: 'You two were arguing last night . . .'

Shit, she thought. 'Did you hear?'

'Not the words,' he said, 'just the pitch . . . Is that why David left?'

She shook her head, relieved. 'Domestic things. Don't worry.' Clearly unconvinced, he patted her shoulder and went inside. She listened for the creak as he climbed into bed beside Baby.

They didn't cook that evening. Baby nibbled, Ann and Christopher ate grilled fish left over from lunch. They sat on the terrace, watching the bats, drinking ouzo from a bottle Ann found in the cupboard. Baby was the first to give in; it was boredom rather than fatigue. 'Time for my beauty sleep,' she cooed.

Ann wondered if she should have gone with David; although she had put on her only dress she still felt dull and ugly. She sat, catching the breeze, willing Christopher to remain with her, dreading the thought that he might do it from pity rather than desire. 'Don't stay out here for me,' she said.

'Don't you want to walk?' he asked.

'I'm perfectly capable of walking on my own.' She didn't mean to sound so aggressive.

'Of course you are,' he replied, 'but I'd like to come along . . .'

Ann blushed. 'Let's go through the vineyard this time, I want to see the house we didn't rent.'

'It would be easier by the road,' Christopher pointed out.

'You can't always take the easy way.' She steered him towards the slope.

The crickets grew silent at their approach. The earth under foot was stony and hard. Christopher held his arm tight round her waist as they stumbled past the dark outlines of outstretched vines. When they reached the house, they found it was just like their own – empty, cheaply furnished, slightly larger – that was all.

'What now?' Christopher queried, 'now that you've risked our necks to get here . . .' For a moment Ann wondered why she was so fond of him.

'Anxious to return to your girlfriend?'

'Not particularly,' he replied.

'Let's sit,' she said. 'Against this vine.'

The ground was warm, sheltered. They sat side by side, their legs splayed out, their backs against the twisted trunk. Seconds passed. Minutes. Ann took Christopher's hand. Stroked it. She turned her face to his. She rolled on top of him, kissed his eyes. Seconds? Minutes? She lifted her dress and made love to him. She was aware, at one point, of a root digging rhythmically into her spine. 'What are we doing?' Christopher whispered, before sinking down on top of her.

Next thing, Ann felt him behind her, his hands on her hips pushing her forward. She complied. He buggered her. He sodomized her, then collapsed on top of her. The root dug into her groin. She squirmed. He got up and helped her to her feet. They walked back along the road without speaking. She savoured the smell of bark and leaves. It was the earth, of course, not Christopher; Christopher had no smell at all.

When they reached the house he turned to her; before he could speak she put her finger to his lips. 'I'm going to sit by the pool,' she whispered. 'You go in.' There was nothing else to say. She slipped off the dress – now damp and stained – and slid into the water. Slowly, it enveloped her. With long, slow strokes she resisted then returned its embrace. She swam till she was exhausted, then hauled herself out and crawled into a chaise.

Later – it was still dark – Christopher came out. He tried to lift her, to carry her in. She refused. He brought out a blanket and covered her. When she next woke it was light. Crows were scratching in the vine. Her body was numb. The sun, cold and red, hung over the field.

Ann was dozing when Baby came out. 'You're up early. Swimming already?' Christopher brought her hot coffee and milk. Baby brought her a thick towel and took her crumpled dress into the house.

Ann lay in her chaise all day waiting for the heat to draw the cold from her bones. That evening David telephoned. He was arriving next afternoon with the boys. They – Ann and David and the boys – would take the stone house in the vineyard. Christopher and Baby could have the farmhouse to themselves. Christopher would propose to Baby; she would accept; they would be married.

Christopher lit the fire that night. Baby made the supper. Ann remained on her chaise until dark, then she went inside and changed into the dress which Baby had scrubbed clean and bleached dry in the sun.

*Famous
Blue
Raincoat*

Jill huddled round the back of the florist watching them put out the rubbish. 'Perfect,' she muttered, snatching a bunch of dead roses from the top of the pile. 'Damn this rain.' She ducked into a dark café; it was two hours yet till the concert, she mustn't get soaked or her voice would dissolve.

Over a mug of sugary tea she composed. 'Dear Lenny . . .' she began. 'Dear Leonard . . .' she began again. 'Dear Leonard Cohen . . .' she finally wrote. 'I own all your albums and sing all your songs. I live in a space near your villa in Greece; we breathe the same air and walk the same streets. I am your soul sister. Meet me tonight at the stage door, I'll be wearing a rose in my teeth . . .' Then she impaled the note on a thorn of the stem and ventured back into the rain.

It was time to phone Dave.

'Why didn't you tell me before?'

'I didn't know about it till this afternoon.' It wasn't true, but if she'd told him about the concert earlier he'd have tried to stop her from going.

'You can't afford the ticket.'

'I'm going without one,' she replied. 'I'm meeting Him after the concert.'

'Don't be ridiculous!' Dave snapped. She hated it when he used this tone. 'How will you get home?'

'I thought maybe you could pick me up.'

'Forget it!'

'Then I'll walk from the station.' She could hear her daughter whimpering in the background. 'Caro? Caro, darling? I won't be late; I'll tuck you in . . .' Before the child could burst into

53

tears she hung up. It wasn't working out with Dave. As soon as she got a job she would find a new place for Caro and her.

She decided to save the bus fare and walk: down Piccadilly, across Knightsbridge, along the Park. Ninety minutes in the rain. She reached the Albert Hall and pushed her way to the artists' entrance. 'I have an important bouquet for the star.'

'Leave it with me, luv,' the doorman yawned.

'I must deliver this missive in person!'

'No one gets backstage without a pass. And you're not allowed to stand in here, miss.'

'I'm not just anyone, you know!'

As he stepped forward to usher her out, she tore a bud from the bedraggled stem then thrust the bunch into his hand and tripped, giggling, back into the storm. She placed the bud between her teeth, retched on the taste, and decided to keep it in her pocket till later.

Security was heavy; it would be impossible to sneak through the door.

Suddenly a man grabbed her arm. 'Miss,' he hissed, 'wanna ticket – cheap?' Fate. It was fate; she was destined to see the concert. She pulled the pound coin from her pocket. It was her train fare home. She grabbed the ticket before he could protest and rushed past the queue to get inside.

The lights flickered. The audience tittered. 'Ssssh!' Jill whispered; they were wasting time. He wouldn't appear until they were silent.

'Ssshhhh!'

'Shush yourself!' someone sputtered. The lights dimmed. *He* appeared. The music rose. He was smaller than she'd imagined; his hair was darker. Dyed? He chatted on between the songs. He chatted too long. 'Let's get on with it!' someone called. 'Come on, Come on!' several voices agreed.

This was too much; this was out of hand. This was Leonard Cohen! 'Shut Up!' she shouted; her voice echoed through the hall: 'Shutup shutup shutup!'

Lenny turned. 'Who?' he answered, 'them or me?' The audience laughed; they were with him again. Because of her joke, they were with him again. She wanted him to sing 'Famous Blue Raincoat', her favourite song, as he well knew.

Suddenly the lights went up: the interval. A security guard peered at her seat, surprised to see it occupied. 'Are you alright?' he asked.

She was shivering. 'Fine,' she smiled, 'I've just got a cold.' She scrabbled around in her bag for a pen. 'Lenny,' she scribbled, 'sing "Famous Blue Raincoat".' Then she scurried up to the stage to add her note to the pile already waiting on the piano.

Back in her seat the security guard was looking at her. 'Do you know Lenny?' she asked. 'I do. We're neighbours in Greece . . . We work together, we collaborate.' This wasn't true, but she did intend to suggest it, so it wasn't really a lie.

The guard edged away. The lights dimmed. The second half of the concert began. Lenny didn't see her note. He played several songs. In a pause between numbers she called out, 'Sing "Famous Blue Raincoat"!' He didn't hear. She shouted again. 'Ssshhh!' people hissed.

Someone tapped her shoulder – the security guard: if she wouldn't be quiet she'd have to leave. Lenny played another song, and another. She couldn't resist, she shouted again, 'Play "Famous Blue Raincoat".' She was shivering, sweating. Lenny came back for two encores. She hurried out before the crowd and ran round to the stage door. Of course – she suddenly realized – he didn't play it on stage because he was going to invite her into his dressing room and play it to her in private.

Jill crouched by the stage door. She was first in line. She was hemmed in by the other fans. She was freezing. But that didn't matter. Soon she would be invited in to Lenny's dressing room. She touched the rosebud in her pocket, the bud by which He would recognize her. The crowd shifted, restless. The guard checked that no one was trying to sneak in.

'He was ever so nice to me last night,' a fat woman cooed, folding up her umbrella. 'He stopped and listened while I told him about my son who's a musician.'

The girl beside her looked anxious. 'I've got three albums for him to sign. D'you think he'll mind? They're not all for me.'

'Oh no, dear, he's ever so polite.'

'He'll be tired tonight though,' a man volunteered. 'Last night of the tour.'

'Eighteen cities in three weeks. Don't know why he does it.'

'For love,' Jill announced. 'He does it for love, you stupid man!'

A blond girl in a tight miniskirt slipped towards the front of the queue. Jill stepped up to stop her when the stage door opened and three men emerged. 'Press,' someone whispered.

'Naw, they're technicians.'

'How long will He be?' Jill demanded.

'Could be forever, for all I know.'

The rain turned to drizzle. 'Can't be long now,' the fat woman crooned, 'he was out in half an hour last night.'

'Tubes stop running in ten minutes,' somebody warned. Several people headed off. Jill didn't mind; Lenny would drive her home anyway.

A dresser came out with a suitcase, then a journalist with a BBC badge, then the musicians with their instruments like bodies stuffed into large, black bags. 'Will he be long?' Nobody replied. A pink limousine cruised by. 'It must be Lenny's!' Half the group rushed after the limo. A few minutes later they returned.

A man emerged in a jacket with 'Leonard Cohen International Tour' on the back. 'Boy, what I wouldn't give for that jacket,' the blond girl sighed.

Jill glared. 'Where is he? We've been waiting an hour!'

'He's gone,' the man replied.

'He wouldn't leave – not Lenny.'

'Some nut's waiting for him. He slipped out the front way ages ago.'

'He wouldn't,' the fat woman muttered. 'He wouldn't desert his fans.' A young man scowled and tore up his programme.

'All the better for me,' Jill thought as she watched the group diminish. 'Fewer people for Lenny to speak to before we can be alone.'

A cab pulled up. The driver dashed through the stage door. The blond girl tried to follow him but was stopped by the security guard. 'Good try,' a man grinned. A few minutes later the driver returned. 'Where is he? Where's Lenny?' He shrugged and roared off, splashing the four remaining fans: Jill, the fat woman, the blond girl, the man.

The woman offered Jill her umbrella; the girl offered her a scarf. Jill refused. Somewhere a bell rang. The security guard turned off the light.

'Isn't he coming?' the fat woman asked as he double-locked the door. The guard pulled up his collar and strode into the rain.

The fat woman put up her umbrella: 'I suppose that's it.' She waddled off.

'Anyone want a lift?' the man asked. The blond girl nodded. Jill listened while their car drove off. Now he would come. She took the rose from her pocket and stuck it between her back teeth. The building was silent. Thunder rumbled in the distance.

A spasm shook her body; she lost her grip, the rose-bud fell into the road and was swept off in a windy gust. Her body was dripping, drooping with cold and fatigue. She wandered round the building. It was empty. It was half past one. The trains had stopped. The traffic had died. She would have to walk home. It would take three hours, maybe four. Caro would still be awake; waiting for her mother to come and tuck her in. Another promise broken . . .

Jill started to walk. Her limbs were numb. The street lights stretched out endlessly, taunting her with greasy grins. Dave was right. They all were right. She was an idiot. She was a failure. She shivered uncontrollably.

Suddenly she heard a man's voice. 'Hey!' She peered through the dark. Then she saw. Across the road. There *He* was. Hunched over his guitar in the rain. She ran forward. He held up his hand. He had a cold. He didn't want to infect her. She mustn't come any closer; he would play from where he stood.

He played 'Famous Blue Raincoat'. He smiled at her. He gazed into her eyes as he sang. He wrapped her in his famous blue raincoat and warmed her from the cold. When the song was over he winked and blew her a kiss. Then he disappeared, melting into the mist. She wanted to follow him, but she had to get back. He wanted her to follow him, to find him, to take him home. But she had other things to do. She had to make tomorrow's audition; she had to get the job, to get the flat for Caro and her. When she had a place of her own, then she would find him and bring him home. She headed down the road; the street lights burned like beacons, she was aflame, she was on fire, she was steaming all the way home.

Manhattan,
New York City,
America,
The World

Two pairs of neatly gloved hands side by side on the wall at the top of the Empire State Building. It's a photograph. I don't remember being there, except for the wind. In the town where we grew up they still believed girls in cities wore gloves. On our first trip to New York – me and my sister and Mum – Mum shopped all over to find the little white gloves for us to wear.

We must have gone to Radio City Music Hall because Mum loved it so much. Going to bed we would beg to hear her descriptions over and over: the dancing girls, the costumes. She had gone every week that year she lived in New York City. The Upper East Side. The school has been turned into a co-op apartment now but the name is still chiselled into the granite: 'The Dobson Ladies' College'.

Mum had rebelled, refused to come out. So Granny had sent her to be finished at this place in New York that a friend of hers recommended. That's where Mum met Andy. Andy is short for Andrea. Andy was a model. And an actress. And she walked dogs and did old ladies' shopping. She did just about anything, but she had her breakfast every morning at the sandwich shop on the corner of Madison and Eighty-Second. That's where Mum first met her. Mum's French tutor was an alcoholic; he often didn't turn up for her morning tutorial, and Mum would disappear to the sandwich shop so he wouldn't get found out.

Because she was an actress Andy knew all the ushers in all the theatres. She and Mum would turn up just as the doors were being closed and slip into empty seats. They saw every show on Broadway that year. The only problem was they never got to see the last act because Mum had to be in by ten. So Andy, who'd seen all the shows several times, would tell Mum the ending on the subway ride home.

The ladies at The Dobson College were not supposed to use the subway, but Mum did when she was with Andy. Then they'd run the five blocks from the subway to the college, but slow down to stroll the final few yards. The ladies at The Dobson College were not supposed to run. Strictly speaking they were not even supposed to walk around the city at night, but Andy was several years older than Mum, and if ever it looked like there would be trouble Andy would put on her sophisticated voice and charm the House Mother.

The first time Andy took Mum out she introduced herself to the House Mother as Mum's American cousin. She said she was a postgraduate student in Literature at Columbia University and that she was taking Mum to a lecture on the Moral Imperatives of the American Folk Tale. After that whenever they were late getting home the House Mother would ask what lecture they'd been to and Andy would reel something off the top of her head while Mum slipped up to her room.

On Saturdays Andy would take Mum to concerts or museums. On Sundays they often went to parties in artists' studios where everyone smoked roll-your-owns and wore black turtleneck sweaters. Sometimes Mum would go back to Andy's apartment for supper. Andy's place was only one room; the kitchen was in one cupboard, the bathroom was in another and the bathtub was in the sitting room with a board across it as a table. There was also a sofa-bed and a window onto the fire escape from which you could hear everyone in the building.

Each time Mum described Andy's apartment it seemed different. On the wall was a huge painting of Andy done by an artist friend. Once Mum said that Andy had no clothes on in the painting, but the next time she left out that detail. When we questioned her, she said that Andy had a red dress on in the painting; another time she said Andy was wearing a black hat with a long, blue feather. Another time she said Andy was stretched out on a red sofa with a blue velvet cloak draped over her body, holding a feather between her teeth.

When Mum's year at The Dobson College was up she returned home to Montreal and married Dad, whose company sent him to Northern Ontario. Every Christmas Andy would send Mum a Christmas card care of The Dobson College, which would forward it to Granny, who would forward it to Mum. Every year Mum would send Andy a letter with our address underlined on the envelope, but somehow Andy kept on loosing the right address.

Then came the year that Mum was supposed to have a baby but she lost it. It was a boy. When Andy's Christmas card came that year Dad said why didn't Mum go and visit her. Dad had never met Andy, but he knew all the stories about her and Mum's year in New York.

At first Mum said no. Then she said what would she do with the girls? Then Dad said the girls should see New York, they were growing up and they should see a little more of the world and Mum owed it to us, if not to herself, to visit the city. So Mum went out one day and bought the gloves for me and my sister, and then we got on a plane and flew to New York.

We went to the Empire State Building because Andy was working at a magazine and wouldn't be free until evening. Then we must have had some lunch, or maybe that's when we went to Radio City Music Hall. Andy had arranged to meet us in the place she always went to after work. But it was a bar, and children weren't allowed inside, so we waited outside while Mum went in to find Andy.

When they came out Andy apologized; she didn't realize children weren't allowed in bars. She hugged us and stepped back and looked at us, then she opened her purse and took out two little bronze Empire State Buildings and handed one to each of us. 'Welcome to Manhattan,' she smiled.

'What's Manhattan?' I asked. I'd never heard the word before.

'Manhattan is here, Manhattan is where you are,' she replied.

'But, Mum,' I cried. Mum wasn't listening. 'But, Mum, you said we were going to New York.'

Andy threw her arms round me. 'Oh darling,' she said, 'oh sweetie.' Then she said to Mum, 'This one reminds me of you. Manhattan is the same as New York,' (she turned back to me), 'it's the same thing, just a different name.'

My sister was jealous so she pretended she'd known all along. 'Didn't you even know that?' she said, but Andy was talking to Mum and didn't notice, so I didn't care.

Andy linked her arm through Mum's and led us through the streets. We were looking for a place to get Coke or ice cream for us – the girls. Mum kept turning round to check on us, but we were following right behind. We wanted to hear what they talked about . . . The Dobson College, the sandwich shop, the baby boy that Mum just lost . . . The traffic noise was always too loud, though, to catch more than a word or two.

Andy was tall. She wore a suit. Mum only ever wore dresses or slacks. Andy had short hair and a little black hat and she smoked cigarettes in a black cigarette holder. We walked and walked and finally Andy said we'd never find anything appropriate in this neck of the woods and we might as well just go back to her place which was right around the corner.

I knew exactly what Andy's place would look like: the smell, the sounds through the fire escape, the painting of Andy on the wall. When Andy opened the door my sister and I both rushed into the room. It was much bigger than it should have been; it had too much furniture. It had three big windows looking onto a park and through the open door at the end you could see a kitchen – a real kitchen, with tables and chairs. 'What about the kitchen in the cupboard,' I whimpered, 'and the bathtub that's a table, and the sofa that you sleep on?'

'Oh, I gave that place up years ago.'

'But why? It was perfect. Mum said it was perfect!'

'Yes, it was perfect,' she smiled at Mum, 'but it was too small.'

'Mum said it was a perfect size; no housework and everything had a place of its own.'

'Yes. But it just got too small.'

'Why?' I persisted.

'Why? Because . . . I was younger then. I had fewer possessions.'

Nobody told me that Andy had moved. It felt like a betrayal. Although I'd never been there before, whenever things got too boring or lonely at home I imagined running away to stay in Andy's place in New York. It didn't matter that I'd never met her; she would welcome me, and then perhaps she'd disappear to walk her dogs and I would walk around the tiny room, and lie on the sofa under the painting of her lying on a sofa, listening to the lives of all the people in the building coming through the window. But that dream was destroyed; this was not the sort of place that one could run away to.

My sister was talking to Andy about school and our dog, answering questions and expanding her answers to sound like grown-up conversation. I knew she was acting, but Mum was pleased. I was too upset to talk. When Andy spoke to me I pretended not to hear, and when Mum said I was being rude Andy laughed and said I was allowed to be rude, in this house anything goes and no one should be forced to answer questions they don't want to. Mum scowled. My sister beamed. I got crosser and crosser because if Andy liked my sister she might invite her to visit on her own. But somehow I couldn't speak anyway; the room was too big and smelled of cigars and there was a pot of ugly orchids in the corner.

While Mum and my sister and Andy were chatting, Andy smoked cigarette after cigarette, taking them from her silver case and inserting them into her thin cigarette holder. Suddenly the lock turned and the door opened and a woman came in. She was older than Mum and Andy. Everyone jumped and Andy hurried over to introduce her. Mum looked a bit nervous as she stood up to shake her hand.

'This is Alex,' Andy introduced her. Alex was short for Alexandra. She was a teacher, a university professor. For a few minutes Mum and Andy tried to make polite conversation, till Alex left to hang up her coat. When she returned she had changed into slacks and was carrying a drink. She tried to be friendly and filled up Mum and Andy's drinks and then went out again. Mum and Andy relaxed when she left.

My sister, full of her triumph with Andy, went into the kitchen where Alex was rattling pans. I knew she would probably get another Coke there, but I couldn't be bothered to follow. I sat in my chair.

'She's in one of her moods,' Mum said when Andy asked me if something was wrong.

'I've got a pain.'

'She's just tired,' Mum replied, 'she hasn't been in a city before.'

'I'm not tired,' I cried, 'I've got a pain.'

'A pain is no fun.' Andy got up. 'Do you want something for it? Can she have an aspirin?'

Mum nodded. 'She has special pills from the doctor but I forgot to bring them.'

'Poor child. Does this happen often?' Andy stroked my forehead.

'It's a phase,' Mum replied. She was cross that I was getting all the attention. I did have a pain. I started to moan. Andy rushed to the bathroom for an aspirin, Mum rushed to the kitchen for a glass of water.

My sister and Alex followed her back. 'It's one of her stomach aches,' my sister announced self-importantly. 'It's alright, she'll get over it after a nap,' she added as Alex bent over me.

Andy gave me the pill and held the water while I swallowed.

'She's got to lie down now,' my sister said, 'that's when the pain goes away.'

'It's not much fun lying down,' Andy said, 'especially when everyone else is still up.' I wanted to hug her for knowing that.

I wanted to stay with her and Mum, but Mum was looking at me. 'Oh pet,' she sighed, 'I thought we were over your stomach aches now.' Then I burst into tears because everyone was being so nice, and I wanted to stay up. But I had to pretend it was the pain that was making me cry so I nodded when Mum said I really should lie down. She and Andy helped me into the bedroom while my sister returned to the kitchen with Alex.

The bedroom was dark. It had a big bed with Alex's hat and Andy's hat and Alex's teaching suit spread across it. Andy hung up the suit in a cupboard while Mum tucked me into the bed. 'Don't worry about supper,' she said, 'you can have a big breakfast tomorrow.'

I cried even more then. 'It hurts,' I said. It didn't, but I wanted to be with the grown ups.

'There, there,' Andy patted my head and pulled the blanket up to my chin. 'In a minute you'll sleep, then your mummy will whisk you back to the hotel and tomorrow you'll wake up and it will be time to go home.' She kissed me on the forehead, then Mum kissed me, then Andy put her arm around Mum and they walked together to the door.

'Wait,' I called as Mum raised her hand to switch off the light.

'What is it, sweetie?' Andy asked.

'Where does Alex sleep?'

Andy shuffled and looked at Mum. Mum looked at the ground.

'Alex doesn't live here,' Andy finally spoke. 'She lives in a different apartment.'

'But her clothes are here.' I knew she lived here, I could smell her cigars on the blanket, mixed with the smell of Andy's perfume.

'You're right,' Andy answered again after a few moments, 'she lives here, this is her home. I live upstairs in the place your mum described to you, the room with the kitchen in the cupboard and the bathtub that's a table.'

'Oh. That's alright then,' I said. 'Can I come and visit you there?'

'Yes, of course. Anytime you like, sweetie,' she said, and blew me a kiss. Then they switched off the light.

I could hear them out there talking and eating and laughing, and I heard my sister laughing too, just like a grown up, but I didn't mind. I was going to visit Andy, any time, in her real apartment. She'd invited me herself. Anytime you like, sweetie.

I dreamed I was sleeping, draped in a red velvet blanket, on Andy's sofa, in her real apartment. She was standing beside me, naked except for her big, black hat and her cigarette holder. The smoke from her cigarette floated up in thin, blue wisps, curling round the edge of her face. And in her arms she held the baby, the lost baby boy, the boy that Mum lost. And I knew that even though I couldn't see her face for the smoke anymore, Andy was taking care of Mum's lost baby boy, and me.

Taboo

jane had cancer of the cervix,
joan had cancer of the breast,
jean had cancer of the colon,
jen had cancer of the chest,
john had cancer of the testicles,
had to have his balls cut off,
jan had cancer of the lymph glands,
poor old jan she had it rough . . .

lousy rhyme.

jill had part of her lung removed,
bill had part of his throat,
will had part of his tongue removed,
phil had part of his . . .

Kay couldn't find a rhyme for throat, so she gave up.

Growth. Growth had the same interior sounds, but that didn't count. Growth. Smoke. Smoking. That did it. Of course there were no ashtrays around. Nobody would be so gauche as to smoke in this place. Primary cancer; secondary cancer: even if you didn't smoke you could pick it up, over the years, sitting on smoky buses, living or working with chronic smokers.

Chronic/acute/degenerative/terminal. Growth, tumour, lump. Neoplasm. She'd just read the word in a medical journal; she wasn't sure what it meant. She wasn't sure she wanted to know.

71

An old man in a bowler hat limped in on a silver-tipped cane. Ignoring the empty chairs in the room, he squeezed up beside the model on the sofa. The babe in the basket beside her gurgled. Great, thought Kay, just what we need, a screaming baby. The baby smiled and went back to sleep. June's babe had been born with a lump on its brain. When it died June developed a tumour in her womb.

The two little boys on the velvet sofa started giggling. They were playing a game, touching each other. It was the sort of game that would never end. It would escalate. Touches would become taps, then jabs, then swipes, then slaps, then hits, then punches, then the mother, deep in her *Times* on the wing chair, would have to step in and stop them. Kay didn't like little boys. Little girls, granted, were often coy. But little boys were menacing. Menacing. Malevolent. No, malignant; malevolent was for people, not things – not diseases. Carcenoma, sarcoma, melanoma, hematoma.

Cyst. Horrible word; though suddenly it sounded benign. Cyst, fibroid, lump. Blood blister. Hard, brutal sounds. Oncologist.

A willowy blond popped her head in the door and nodded to the model. Swinging her long hair over her shoulder she scooped up the sleeping babe and swept out to join her friend in the foyer. She wasn't there in her own right; she was just waiting. For a friend.

Oncologist. Yes. Hard words. Charlatan, quack, hakim, sorcerer, medicine man. Witch doctor. Specialist. Doctor. Oncologist.

Funny how doctors in private practice felt the need to establish their social credentials. Like the minister in her husband's church when they'd gone to meet him before the wedding. What school? What college? What hobbies, games, sports? What books, plays, operas (OPERAS!!)? What sort of

music – classical of course, but which composers in particular . . . Her last meeting – which was also her first meeting
– with a private doctor had been the same. A twenty minute
consultation, three quarters of which was concerned with who
she knew and where she lived and what she did. And what her
husband did. And her parents, and his parents. And then after
a cursory look he'd rung up another specialist.

Her GP simply asked when she'd noticed it, whether it
hurt, whether there was a history of (momentary pause –
was this to build up the suspense, or was he searching for
a euphemism?) CANCER (pause to let the word sink in) in
the family.

Of course there was. Of course there is. Every family
has its cancers. Her paternal grandmother died of stomach
cancer, but meals were always such a trauma in that house
it was hardly surprising. Her paternal grandfather died of
throat cancer, but he talked too much. Not talked, shouted.
He didn't like children; not his own, not his offspring's. They
were all secretly pleased when he kicked off. Poetic justice,
her mother had muttered when the disease was first mooted.
Her mother's own mother died of pneumonia, which was only
named cancer after her death. Her maternal grandfather had
died in the war; he didn't live long enough to claim a cancer
of his own.

Kay's mother had had an emergency hysterectomy ten years
ago. But that had been a response to having her youngest – and
only son – leave home. Kay was a little peeved at the time at how
obvious it was. Utterly and characteristically unimaginative.
Besides which, it proved, as Kay always maintained, that the
son was the favourite. Certainly there was no question of her
mother contracting cancer when she or her two sisters left.
Contracting cancer. Developing cancer. Discovering cancer.
Inventing cancer. Cancercancercancer. The Big C.

'S. Grey.' She jumped. The short-haired woman in the
black leather jacket stood up and strode out. Cancer of
the heart, Kay thought; it looks like it's all eaten up. Kay's
friend Karen, married to a stockbroker, had cervical cancer last

year: self-punishment for those three monstrous sons she had passed into the world.

'Miss Brown.' The receptionist's voice was hypnotic. A tiny prune-like woman pulled herself forward on arms like elastics. The chair she vacated was pounced on by the quickest of the little boys. Miss Brown, Kay thought, why are you a Miss (hit/miss) after all these years? Miss Brown, do you suffer paroxysms of humiliation when the hearty doctor violates your wry little frame with his prying eyes? Miss Brown, we have spent thirty minutes together without exchanging a word. Will we ever meet again? And to what shattering revelations are you now prey or party, Miss Brown?

Oh, I'm sure you have nothing to worry about. Miss? Mrs? Mizz? – surely you're not one of those bitter women. We'll just take a look. Hmmm. Aaaah. Ahaaa. A spot, shadow, haze, maybe on the plate. Very interesting. Don't know for sure. Can't tell you yet. Professionals don't predict. More tests. I'll send you along to my friend Doctor X, Doctor X-ray. X, Y, Z. I'm sorry, dear. Dear! Can't be more definite. We'll take another look at the tests. I'll make an appointment. Wait. Another appointment. Wait. My friend Doctor X. Best in the business. Two or three months. He's a busy man. Wait.

Kay's father insisted she go private this time.

'Mrs White.' The receptionist's bland, magnolia voice wafted through. Mrs White. Was illness a prerogative of womanhood? Mrs White. Miss Brown. The mother and sons. The striped-shirt woman. The short-haired S. Grey. And Kay. And what of the little old man, drowsing on his silver-tipped cane? He didn't count.

Mrs White, demure in her blossom-sprigged dress with matching blue shoes, travelled up from the country this morning, wearing her best daddy-please-doctor-don't-hurt-take-care-of-me-make-it-all-better dress. Scurrying out, she tripped on the threshold, almost losing her matching blue bag. Kay wished she had smiled sympathetically when Mrs White looked at her earlier in her startle-eyed sweep of the room. At the time she had simply stared stonily on.

74

A calm, complacent air seemed to settle in after Mrs White's exit. The old man shook himself awake and smiled to the room at large. The boy in the chair was reading a magazine, mouthing the words as he went. His brother was playing with a plastic puzzle, sliding silver bubbles into the too-small rim of a champagne bottle, encased in a disc the size of a fifty pence piece. The boys were sweetly self-absorbed, so their mother put down her paper to dream.

Sara had a lump on her breast. It was removed but then proved benign. Sian had the wrong breast removed by mistake. Suzie had a lumpectomy, but proclaimed that next time she'd have the whole thing off, both of them for good measure, damned things. Breasts, bosoms, boobs, bazookas, tatas, tits, udders, mammaries, mounds.

Jack had the spot on his lung and survived. Jack's mother had died of some sort of cancer but no one could quite remember which. Jill had a dodgy smear last year; she went vegetarian and three months later they pronounced her clear. John had sworn by the Bristol diet. But he'd died anyway. Jack's wife had the lump removed from her cheek, then the second one from the side of her face. They said they were safe, but best to be sure. The scars were larger than the lumps had been. But it's best to be sure. Clair had leukaemia. Suddenly, in middle age. She was dying, but no one admitted it.

After the chemo Lynne's hair all fell out. She looked sicker now though, with the jet black wig. She'd been grey for decades; must not have noticed. Curious thing: self-image, vanity. Other than that though she seemed alright. Recovering. State of remission. (You never recover.)

Mrs Black was called. And Matthew and Mark. The boys bustled out self-importantly, not waiting for their mother who straggled, struggling to fit her oblong newspaper into her square shoulder bag.

Now there was only Kay and the old man. He seemed to be sleeping, head resting on his crossed hands on the silver-topped cane. He seemed to have all the time in the world. Well he would, wouldn't he? When you got to that age what did it matter? Cancer, pneumonia – what's in a name?

Gemma had to have her ovaries removed when she was seventeen. Gemma's neighbour, Mrs Flannagan, was recovering from her radiation. She still mourned the missing bit of liver, but physically she looked fine. Unlike her son Billy who had a chunk cut out of his lip. What did you expect after twenty years' worth of nicotine sticks hanging off it? His brother Pat had a spot on his lung. And Andy had throat cancer. A family of smokers. But their grandmother, old Lady Mott, smoked a pipe all her life out behind the barn. And she was still living.

Just goes to show, Kay thought to herself. It just goes to show. You never can tell.

'Ms Green,' the receptionist called. The old man jerked his head off his hands, looked around, then dropped off.

You could go on like this forever, Kay thought. You could fill pages, chapters, whole books with the lists of the people with cancer. Those who died. Those who survived. Those few who made miraculous recoveries. Those many who slowly declined, sometimes so slowly that something else got to them first.

And then there were the cancer scares, the ones who were convinced they had it and didn't. The ones who died a dozen deaths each time they found a lump or a bump or an unexplained pain. 'Ms Green,' the receptionist called again.

The old man didn't bother to stir himself and feign consciousness. Kay gathered her things and headed for the door.

Author's
Tour

She grew up in a small, affluent English town in Canada's French-speaking province of Quebec. She went to the right university, which was full of Americans exploiting the Ivy League reputation at half the Ivy League price. Then she got an overseas scholarship to take her M.A. in English Literature at the London School of Economics. There she met the person who soon became her husband, and settled down to life as an expatriate in London. After several years, she achieved moderate success as a poet. When her third collection was put out by a recognized British publisher she was invited by the Arts Council to do an author's tour of Canada.

Midway through her reading in a tiny bookshop in Montreal she looked up and saw a man she recognized from her student days. He slipped through the door and slid into one of the empty chairs at the back of the room. She remembered that he was someone she had once slept with. Quickly she adjusted the patter on the poem she was about to read; it was one of those versatile poems about an unsatisfactory relationship which could have been written about almost any affair, but, as it happens, was written about none in particular.

'This is about a man I knew . . . or thought I knew . . . many years ago, in this city. In those days my mother used to say,' she said – and this, in fact, was true – 'it's not the morality of hopping into bed with just anybody which bothers me, it's that you kids hurt each other so casually. And somebody always gets hurt.' Then she read the poem. It was duly applauded, and she wrapped up the reading several minutes early.

The man waited by the door while the audience surged round her. Finally, when the signing ended, when everyone drifted off clutching his or her unique observations, when the publisher's rep had settled accounts with the owner of the shop, finally she approached him. I have made it, she assured herself, I live in London, England, I am a poet, I am a married woman . . . .

She shook his hand. He kissed her cheek. Both cheeks. Ten years ago it had seemed a sophisticated greeting. Now she and her circle kissed each other once, on the lips, to prove, perhaps, they weren't afraid of Aids. 'You wear your hair out now,' he said. 'I always said you should.'

'Do you still live on Rue Milon?' she asked, knowing, suddenly that he would, wishing she could think of something less banal to say. 'This is . . . ah . . . my publisher,' she said. 'Can you join us for a meal? Afterwards I'll walk you home; we can catch up on things.'

After dinner in a Greek restaurant which she remembered from the early days, they headed off. 'Don't forget; Windsor Station at ten tomorrow,' the publisher's rep reminded her as she climbed into the Volvo. Ten years ago he had sworn he'd never own a car.

From the outside, his flat was just as she remembered; it sat in a seedy district of Victorian houses defaced by Russian furriers and Polish bakeries. The brutalism of steel and glass which had recently swept the city had left the neighbourhood with an almost fashionable air of fifties' retro. As they tackled the four flights of stairs to his flat she noticed that the stink of urine had given way to a smell of paint. 'The German sisters who lived next door were succeeded by a professor,' he explained.

'I see,' she nodded, squeezing round his ten-speed bike as he struggled with the key.

'Do you still drink?' he asked as they spilled into the kitchen. 'You didn't have much at dinner.'

'I wanted to be sober. At least till we got back here.'

She looked around. It had hardly changed. 'I've been trying to remember what the place looks like. I can picture the bedroom . . . (There wasn't much to it, she thought to herself, it was always dark) . . . The sitting room with that sofa you were so proud of . . .'

'Beidermeyer,' he said, proudly.

'. . . And this table,' she continued. Old pine. He'd bought it before pine became fashionable; at least that's what he always said. 'But I can never remember what's in the room next to the bathroom. Over the years it has plagued me. When I think about it,' she added quickly, 'which isn't all that often.' She could do a complete tour of the flat in her mind, room by room, item by precious item. But she always came up short at that door. She twisted round; there it was, the door beside the bathroom. As always in her mental picture, it was shut.

'It's my study,' he said.

'Is it possible that I never went inside it?' she asked.

'There's nothing to see; my desk, papers, books, that's all. And the window to the fire escape. Take a look if you like. I'll open a bottle.'

'Later,' she said. 'I'm too tired.' She sat while he poured two glasses of wine. Thick. Viscous.

He pulled out a chair and faced her. 'To . . .' he hesitated, lifting his glass. 'To . . .'

'Old friends?' she offered. He shook his head. 'Loose ends? Unfinished business?'

'To old wounds,' he proclaimed, saluting her.

She let the rich, red acid crawl round her mouth, over the lump of her heart which threatened revolt in her throat, down the suddenly empty pit of her stomach. He lifted her leg stretched out beside him; slipped off the sandal, squeezed her foot in a gesture he'd perfected a decade before. She loved having her foot squeezed. 'Freudian,' he'd pronounced when she first admitted it. 'Foot equals penis . . . Cinderella and all that jazz.' She realized, then, that he went to a shrink.

But all that was in the past. Suddenly she was terribly, utterly tired. 'Spend the night,' he suggested. She was too exhausted to refuse. She stumbled into the bathroom while he washed the dirty glasses. He never could leave an ashtray, a glass, an empty bottle out of place. She debated using his toothbrush – he had always been so fastidious, if she asked he'd probably object; if she used it anyway he'd notice it was wet. She asked.

'Sure,' he replied.

'You're sure?' she asked again, surprised.

'When you consider the places we put our mouths, a used toothbrush is nothing.' He winked at her in the mirror on his way to run her a shower. Hot. He remembered she liked it hot. Then he left her alone in the bathroom, leaving the door slightly ajar.

She stood in the shower wondering why the layout of this flat had worried her over all these years. There had been other affairs; all of them had lasted longer than this one. She tried to recall how long they'd been together. A week perhaps. Hardly an affair. How often could they have made love? Once? Twice perhaps? While she was musing, he came in and began to undress. His body was even tighter, leaner than she remembered. She backed out of the steam to watch him. He stepped into the shower and pulled her to join him. She resisted. 'You're too hard for me. You always were,' she added, shielding her rounded belly with both arms. 'You still seeing your analyst?' she asked. He nodded. 'And you still prefer to live alone?' Again, he nodded. 'Is that older woman still around? Genevieve? She was French, wasn't she?'

'Is. We're still together. Sometimes. Sometimes not.' He soaped himself, thoroughly, meticulously, every crack and crevice down to the gaps between his toes. 'Is it true that English men don't wash?' She ignored the question.

'Did you ever tell her about me?' she asked. 'I suppose there was no point, I mean we were hardly an issue, were we – you and me; I mean it was hardly a threat to whatever you had with her, was it?'

'Are you kidding?' He dropped the soap. 'We were together for months, you and me. You met all my friends: Rob and Christopher and Lise . . . They all know you by name. You must remember!'

Suddenly she did remember. Dinner parties. One with a Rhodes scholar back from Cambridge for the 'Michaelmas' break. And another one, full of people, which ended late at night on the mountain, sliding on trays, in the dark, through the snow, down the mountain. God, it was fun: the sheer release – the terror of it.

So, she thought, he must be right: two dinner parties at least. Maybe they'd been together for a month. But where were the nights? She only remembered one. One endless night of grinding and all she had wanted was sleep. She remembered thinking at the time, Is this what they call performance, or is he having trouble getting it up? Maybe there had been other nights. Maybe that was just the first; or the last; or maybe all the nights had been the same, so it had only seemed like one.

Perhaps, she thought, perhaps her memory was at fault. But over these ten years it had been that single, endless night – that's all she had been able to recall of the relationship. And when she'd tried to make sense of it, all she saw was his body, his hard, sleek body grinding into her.

'Hey,' he said, enveloping her in a towel – the steam was blurring everything – 'hey, babe,' he held out his hand to her, 'you're swaying.'

She shivered. 'I think I'm cold. I think I had too much to drink.'

'You always did,' he smiled.

'Did I?'

She let him lead her into the bedroom. The light was on. The room was dark. 'Let's open the curtains,' she said, 'I can't sleep in a room with the curtains closed.'

'There are no curtains,' he replied, steering her to the bed.

The rest was a blur: red wine, sleep, the pillows too deep, under the duvet she smothered, out of it she froze, and there wasn't enough room. And when she curled towards the warm, familiar body of her husband he wasn't there and she dreamed of him – her lover – grinding, grinding into her and she opened her eyes. The room was dark. Grey. Yellow. And there he was, staring at her.

'Do you remember,' he said, 'the first time we made love you were bleeding.'

'Was I? Why?'

'It was, you know, you had your period.'

'Oh,' she replied. 'Did I really? How disgusting.' He kissed her forehead and leapt out of bed. He really does leap, she thought to herself.

'Headache?' he asked. She nodded. He left the room and returned a few minutes later with – she knew it would be – two glasses of fresh orange juice, and an aspirin.

'What time is it? Is it night?' she asked.

'Eight o'clock.'

'What!' She jumped. 'It can't be. It's still dark!'

'No it isn't,' he pointed to the hall beyond the open door. A shaft of sunlight bounced off the polished floor.

'Oh my God!' She jumped up, 'I've got to be at . . .'

'. . . Windsor Station at ten,' he finished her sentence. 'No problem. I'll drive you. Take it easy; there's plenty of time.' She fell back in the bed and stretched. 'We have two hours,' he calculated. 'An hour and a half really, less half an hour to get there; that leaves one hour; less thirty minutes to wash and dress, fifteen minutes for "contingencies" . . .' he looked meaningfully at her. She groaned. He shrugged. '. . . That makes fifteen minutes for the aspirin to take effect.'

He sat on the bed stroking her forehead. 'Will you come back through here on your return to London?' He said the word 'London' with reverence. He was that kind of snob.

'I fly from Toronto, I'm afraid.'

'I'm going to Paris this winter; I could come via England.'

'You could stay with us,' she said.

'Us,' he mimicked. 'No,' he muttered, 'I'm going with Genevieve anyway.'

'Both of you could stay with us.' She wondered what her husband would make of this man. She wondered if he'd guess that they had once been lovers. Would she tell him? What would she say? We were lovers once. Once: I mean one time. That's all I remember anyway. One time ten years ago. Maybe she wouldn't tell him, she thought. Maybe he wouldn't ask.

'Ten past eight,' he announced, slipping his tight little buttocks into a pair of baby blue jockey shorts.

'Will you open the curtains?' she asked, 'I can't get up until I see what sort of day it is.'

'No curtains to open,' he replied, pulling on a neat, pressed shirt. 'This room has no windows; don't you remember?'

'No windows? You can't have a bedroom with no windows!'

'My study is really the bedroom,' he said. 'But I've always used this room instead.'

'So even when I . . . when we . . . when I used to sleep here,' she persisted, 'there were never any windows?'

'Never.'

'Christ . . . I can't – I never could – sleep in a room that has no windows.'

Slowly she got herself up and dressed to the semi-light of the sun in the hall outside. He drove her to the station. They arrived early. He didn't wait with her for the train. He didn't visit her in England that winter. She didn't explain to her husband about this man who was her lover once, ten years before, in a room without any natural light. No windows to close, no curtains to open. And another room which she'd never even entered.

*Katherine
the Great*

Katherine the Great lived upstairs from me. 'The Great' was my addition; to her friends she was simply Kate. I don't know if you'd call her a nymphomaniac, but Katherine was certainly pretty voracious. At night my ceilings sighed with bodies bouncing up and down. On weekends the front door bell cried her steady stream of visitors: sometimes two or three in an evening; they would pass on the stairs, one in, one out, nodding sympathetically as two who share a secret vice.

Don't get me wrong; she wasn't a hooker. Katherine was a researcher for the BBC. Occasionally she'd come down for a cup of tea. She was well versed in current affairs: 'Have you heard the news about Aiden Quinn? And of course you know McKellan's gay? And what about the new Gere film! That profile can't be real, can it; perhaps he's had an implant.

Personally, she preferred younger men: Michael Jackson, Michael Fox. She went to see *Bright Lights* four times. Her lovers, though, were odd-looking chaps: very thin or over-weight; some were balding in their thirties, others looked like foetuses or wizened old men. They were writers and actors and film-makers. One worked in the city, but he didn't last long.

The lucky ones got to walk out with her in the mornings. When we met up at the front door, she would always introduce me: 'This is my best friend,' she would say, 'a flautist.' She pro-nounced it 'flute-ist'. The ones who'd been before remembered my name. 'Hi, kid,' they'd quip, 'how's the music biz?' They made a point of remembering me – anything to give them a foothold, a claim at belonging, a whisper of permanence. I was part of the set-up for them, the little musician on the ground floor.

I couldn't distinguish them one from another: Ben and Bill and Joe and John – they were all the same to me. But I smiled politely to each one, benevolent as Katherine herself. Oh, she was benevolent, in her way. No one was favoured; she spread herself fairly. When one or another seemed to be getting too involved she'd come in with a worried frown: 'George is becoming a problem,' she'd say. 'He can't handle this sort of relationship. I explained it to him at the beginning, but he wants some kind of commitment. I'll just have to give him the shove, I'm afraid. Men these days; such emotional cripples. All they want is security. They haven't heard of liberation.' (When she was eight, Katherine's father had gone off to join the sexual revolution. He had never come home.) And after a few plaintive phone calls George would hover – perhaps glimmer for an instant as his soft underbelly, rolling, flickered in the sun. Then he'd sink from view forever.

Life went on in much the same way, month after month. I graduated from the Academy and joined the Philharmonic. Katherine moved around in the Beeb: Talks and Features for a while, then onto Light Entertainment. Sometimes her lovers would ring up and talk to me when she wasn't in. Some even came to my concerts. Then later, at the pub, they'd bring the conversation round to her: 'What's she up to these days? Shame; I hoped she'd be here. Tell her you saw me, eeh? There's a good kid.' And they'd be off. I suppose they thought we were closer than we were. Though we were pretty close. I suppose.

One night, it was early spring, there was a commotion in the hall: a clatter of three or four men in tap shoes tripping up the stairs. This is odd – I thought, sipping my tea in front of the Thursday evening film – she's usually pretty strict about only having one in at a time. But the noise stopped at the top of the stairs, so I thought no more about it.

Later though, much later, in the middle of the night, an almighty thud sounded from above. It shook the ceiling, it shivered the walls, it shattered the dishes piled in the sink; it resounded though the house and silence echoed in its wake. The noise had come from Katherine's room. I lay in the dark for several minutes wondering what to do. Finally, there was nothing else for it; I dragged on my dressing gown and went to investigate.

When I opened her door the place was a shambles: the bed was broken in two places, the dressing table was overturned, the books were scattered about the floor. Then I saw her. Pinned. Naked. Flat as a pancake, dead as a dishrag, under a large and terrified horse. In the excitement it must have lost its balance. It lay across her, nostrils flaring, legs splayed foolishly about it like a skirt. I hauled the sweating beast to its feet taking care that it didn't step and leave a hoofprint in her flesh. After a lot of prodding I managed to coax it down the stairs and shove it out into the night.

When Katherine didn't turn up for work, they sent someone to investigate. Her face, when they found it, was smiling. 'Funny,' they told me, 'you wouldn't believe it, but right by the bed was a pile of horse manure.' Later, when the police came round and asked if I'd seen anything odd I said, 'Nothing unusual' . . . I mean, what can you say?

The
Storyteller

'It's him,' Mark scowled, handing her the telephone. 'I thought you weren't going to see him again!' He grabbed his briefcase and left, slamming the door behind him.

For weeks she'd meant to stop seeing Lewis. 'The problem is,' she'd explained to Mark, 'he doesn't have any friends in this country.'

'That's not your problem.'

She'd shrugged: 'People respond to a need.'

'Not people, suckers. He's using you!'

'Besides,' – why was she defending him? – 'besides, he tells me stories.'

'If you want to see him, far be it from me; I haven't even met the bloke. *You* keep saying what a pain he is. *You* said he depresses you . . .'

'He does. He is. You're right,' she'd replied, vowing once again to end it.

A few minutes later the doorbell rang. 'I have a great idea for a story,' Lewis announced, walking straight past her into the kitchen, pouring himself a mug of tea, 'the problem is, I'm afraid it might be sexist.'

'Then it probably is.'

The problem is, she thought to herself, he's a much better writer than me. She was a sucker for talent and this boy – he was five years younger – this boy was clearly talented.

'The story goes . . .' he parked himself on the table, picked

95

a crust from Mark's plate and dipped it in the marmalade jar, 'I was out last night with Joy . . .' he paused to scrape his crust across the butter. Joy was a leggy Colombian model he'd picked up in a bar recently. 'I was out with Joy last night, and she offered to cook dinner. I'm dead broke so I jumped at it; it's the first time she's invited me. So we get to her apartment and she spends all the time telling me about her former lover, this guy called Joe.'

'I dare say there have been many,' she observed.

'This one was also American, also a writer – an old man though, in his forties. Anyway, she goes on about how she despises the guy; she even gets out her album to show me photos. He's not bad-looking, I must admit, but – '

'Where's the story?'

'I'm coming to it. Anyway, she cooks dinner . . .'

'What does she cook?'

'I don't know, vegetables – in a wok – '

'Is she vegetarian?'

'I guess she must be.'

'Figures,' she muttered.

Lewis ignored this comment. 'So we're sitting side by side on the couch . . . and we run out of wine. So I go round to the liquor store, and when I get back she's taken off her clothes. She's sitting there, nothing on but her panties. Well, I figured something sexual was on the cards, but I hadn't expected it to be quite so soon . . . So I sit down beside her and she starts whispering things in my ear.'

'What sort of things?'

'Dirty things. Things she wants me to do to her.'

'And . . .?' He grinned, teasing her. 'Did you do them?' she persisted.

He shook his head.

'Why not?'

'I get the feeling she didn't really want them. She's just saying it. Besides,' he winked, 'some of the things are illegal.' He paused for a moment then proceeded. 'So anyway, we're stroking each other and things. I have my pants off by this time, to keep her company. And suddenly she jumps up and shouts, You're just using me!'

'And?'

'That's it. It's a bit of a passion killer. So I get up and put on my pants. We kiss each other on the lips. And then I go. It's two in the morning so I have to walk all the way home.'

'Where's the story?' she asked, annoyed, but not sure why.

'Well,' he leaned towards her. 'The story is about this woman who begs a man to do weird things to her. When he refuses she accuses him of rape.' He spoke the final word as though the word itself were taboo. Then he sat back, like some satisfied Pasha surveying the source of his pleasure.

'I think it's a horrible story. It's utterly implausible; it sounds like bad pornography. And you're right,' she announced, 'it *is* sexist.' She grabbed his mug, threw the unfinished tea down the sink.

Lewis could see he was unlikely to cajole her into a good mood. 'Can I use the phone?' He pulled it towards him; 'I promised Joy I'd ring.'

'Use the box on the corner, I'm expecting a call.'

'Ooh. Must be important . . .'

'It is,' she replied. 'The BBC.'

'Oh,' he muttered, and left in a sulk.

She didn't usually discuss work with Lewis, but she knew her commissions irked him. He couldn't see that diligence and reliability were as important as sheer talent. He assumed that the world should come to him – as indeed it would, she thought ruefully – but until it did, she could indulge in the occasional poke at his swollen ego. As she closed the door behind him, she vowed that next time Lewis called she would make some excuse to avoid him.

But here he was, again, on the phone. 'Are you busy?' he asked. She could hear from the background noise he was ringing from the café on the corner.

'It's nine o'clock in the morning; of course I'm busy.' She resented his indolence almost as much as his arrogance.

'I have to talk.'

'I have a meeting.'

'It won't take long?'

He would probably turn up anyway. 'Fifteen minutes. That's all.' He hung up without even thanking her.

Before she'd finished gathering her notes he was on the front step. He didn't appear as upset as he'd sounded. He nodded towards her pile of papers: 'Serious meeting?'

'Mmm,' she led him firmly past the kitchen and into the study. 'So, what is it?'

He waited till she was sitting. 'Remember I told you about Monday night with Joy?' She nodded. 'Well, this morning I got a call from a man who says he's a friend of the family.' He paused a moment, then proceeded. 'He says Joy's accused me of rape.'

'What!'

He nodded.

'I see,' she replied.

'She must have flipped out.'

'Why now? Why with you?'

'Must be something to do with this other man. Joe, her other American lover. She kept telling me how she hated him; I guess she must have made some connection between him and me.'

'How extraordinary.' She couldn't think of another thing to say.

Lewis continued. 'He must have made her do things she didn't want to do.'

'How do you know?'

'She told me,' he replied, irritated.

'What sort of things?'

'Now you sound like the guy on the phone.'

'Who is he, anyway, this man? What business is it of his?'

'A family friend. He might be a lawyer or something; he seemed very calm. He kept asking me questions. What were you wearing? What was she wearing? What colour? Where were your hands at this point? At that point? What did you do? What did she do?'

'And you answered him?'

'I explained that the whole thing was ridiculous, that nothing happened, that she must be mad. I told him she kept asking me to do things . . .'

'Did you tell him what things?'

'He asked; I told him. Then he said – he was nice about it – he said he would get back to me.'

It was nearly half past nine. 'Do you think he believed you?'

'I don't see why not. He seemed like a reasonable person.'

'Look, Lewis, I'm sorry,' she said. 'I really have to go. It could be worse; the man – what's his name? – '

'He didn't say.'

'You didn't ask?'

'I didn't think to . . .'

'No, of course. Now I must . . .'

'I hate the idea of going back to that cold little room . . .' he interrupted.

'Come on, Lewis,' she gathered her papers, wishing she'd had time to jot a few notes for the morning's meeting. Before he could ask to stay she ushered him out and locked the door behind them.

Later, returning on the tube, she wondered if Lewis was capable of rape. She could imagine him convincing someone to do things they didn't want to – persuading, cajoling, defeating by sheer tenacity; but the idea of Lewis physically overpowering anybody . . .? She decided not to discuss it with Mark.

The next morning when the telephone rang she knew it would be him. 'Hello?' She picked up the receiver.

'He called again.' (Not 'Hello', or 'How are you', or 'Hi, this is Lewis'.)

'And?' she replied.

'Can I come round?'

'No, Lewis; I have a script to finish.'

'What script?' he queried, petulant.

'For the BBC.'

'Oh.'

'I told you about it.'

'I must have forgotten.'

'I dare say you did.' (Fuck you, she thought.)

'He called again.'

'Yes, you said.'

'He said she's changed her story.'

'Good.'

'It isn't as bad as it was; now she's just claiming I forced her into oral sex.'

'That isn't as bad as rape?'

'Apparently not.'

'I see.' She paused; he didn't speak. 'How do you account for the change?'

'Well I know she's touchy about her mouth; she doesn't like being kissed on the lips, so something must have happened; the old boyfriend must have forced something on her.'

'What do you mean, she doesn't like being kissed on the lips?'

'She turns away.'

'But you told me last week, you said that you kissed each other on the lips. I remember – it seemed a strange detail to include.'

'So I kissed her,' he exploded. 'I tried to kiss her on the lips, she turned her face, so I kissed her cheek. What's this, the third degree? I mean, Jesus Christ! You're the only person I can talk to in this goddamned country. Don't you believe me either?'

'No, Lewis,' she spoke with exaggerated calm. 'I do not think you raped this woman. Now what do you think is behind it all?'

'For Christ's sake! I don't know! The woman's mad. She's a kid: she's a child. Obviously this man Joe forced her to perform oral sex. She'd probably never even heard of it and she was scared.'

'A twenty-three-year-old woman is hardly a child; and nobody who watches TV after eight in the evening can not know about oral sex.'

'She's not twenty-three,' he replied, 'she's nineteen.'

'You told me she was twenty-three.'

He paused a moment. 'Well she must have told me that. But the man on the phone said she's only nineteen. Look, can't I come round? I'm really distraught.'

She was tempted to end it all then and there, but she didn't want him to think that she believed he was a rapist; she sensed that it would give him some satisfaction which she wasn't prepared to give. 'No, I must go; I have work to do.'

'Wait a minute!' he implored, then he continued slowly. 'I told the man on the phone – I explained that Joy must be transferring something from this Joe character onto me. I told him how she despised the guy, how she kept on saying how she hated him.'

'And?'

'Nothing. He said he'd get back to me . . .'

'When?'

'When he feels like it; how should I know.'

It was almost noon. She had to get the script to the producer by six. 'This man sounds creepy; you should get his name. Tell him *you'll* ring *him* next time.'

'Oh sure,' Lewis snapped. 'Antagonize the guy. Very clever. He could go to the cops; that's the last thing I need.'

'What difference does it make, if you're innocent!'

'Come off it!' he scoffed. 'You don't think they're going to believe me, a Yank, over some frail little girl and her family lawyer!'

'She's hardly a little girl, at six feet!'

'Joy isn't six foot. What makes you think that? She's about five five.'

'You told me she was six feet tall,' she answered, quietly.

'Well she says she is. She'd like to be.'

'How can she be a model if she's only five foot five?'

'She hasn't had that many jobs,' he replied sulkily.

'And *is* she Colombian?'

'Yes. I told you she is.'

'And coffee coloured? With legs that go up to the sky?'

'What are you being so snide about?'

'Lewis, I'm busy. I have to go.'

'But what about me? What will I do?'

'Wait for his next call.'

'Thanks. Thanks a lot,' he slammed down the phone.

'Thank God for that, she thought, returning to her desk.

That night as she and Mark lay in bed, the telephone rang. The last time the phone had rung after midnight it had been her father announcing her brother's accident. At dawn he had rung again to say that her brother was dead.

Mark switched on the light and reached across her for the phone.

'Hello,' he said in his calmest voice. She watched him. His face froze. Silently he handed her the receiver.

'Hello?' her voice trembled. It was Lewis.

'Joy just telephoned,' he said, 'she was livid, she was crazy. She screamed at me, she screamed, Why did you tell Joe the things I said about him? Apparently the man on the phone was Joe – her lover, her American lover, the man who said he was a family friend . . . I thought I detected an accent . . .'

Mark rolled over, kicking her as he went, pulling the covers over his head. She didn't want him to know about the rape. 'So what are you saying?' she finally asked quietly, carefully, into the phone.

'It must be some sort of hoax; they must be in it together.'

'Hmm,' she replied. 'I'll speak to you in the morning.'

'Did I ring too late?' he asked: hurt innocence. 'Joy just got off the phone and I had to discuss it with somebody . . .'

'I'll speak to you tomorrow,' she repeated, then hung up.

Mark was silent. She tried to ease some blankets back. He wasn't releasing any. She turned off the light and curled up beside him, relieved, at least, that he hadn't asked about the call. 'I thought you were going to get rid of him,' he muttered through the bedding.

'I am. Tomorrow. I thought I had.'

'What does he want at this time of night?'

'It's too complicated.' She risked a vague reply, calculating that Mark would be too proud to push. She was right. He didn't move. He pretended to sleep. Eventually he did sleep. She freed some of the bedclothes and finally fell asleep herself.

The next morning she was startled awake by the phone ringing; Mark had gone, slipping out early. It was Lewis. 'I think I know what's going on,' he said as she picked up the receiver.

'So do I,' she replied.

'What?' he asked.

'Lewis, I don't want to hear anymore of your story. I don't care.'

'What?' His voice had a hint of panic. 'It isn't a story; it's my life.'

'I don't want to hear any more, Lewis. No more of your life, no more of your story, no more of you at all.' There was silence. 'Do you understand?' He didn't reply. 'This is it, Lewis.' Still he didn't speak. 'I haven't time for you. I don't want to see you; I don't want to hear from you.' She could hear him breathing down the line. 'Do you understand; this is about *me*.' Silence. 'Lewis, I'm going now.'

Slowly, quietly, she put down the receiver. A few minutes later she picked it up and listened. He was gone. She took the phone off the hook and got out of bed. On her way to the kitchen she double-locked the front door. Then she made herself a pot of tea and moved into the study to work on the story she had begun.

La Bocca
Della
Verita

Things weren't going well between Wendy and Jim. The decision to move in together seemed to give rise to all sorts of problems. Sure, they'd been lovers for three years, but when it came to the crunch, Jim was afraid they'd get bored with each other. It wasn't that he didn't love her. And God knows – God forbid! – there wasn't anyone else. And of course it was mad to pay for two places since they spent at least five nights a week together. It was those last two nights, he supposed. And as spring drew on he seemed to stretch those two nights into three, and sometimes even four. So when Wendy's friend Xavier wrote from Rome she decided to visit him. Far from being jealous at this uncharacteristic bid for separation, Jim thought it was a great idea. 'A weekend in Rome might be just the thing,' he crooned. 'You've been a bit peaky recently.'

Wendy had met Xavier on a walking tour of the city. She wasn't the walking tour type, but one Saturday while waiting for Jim in a pub she'd noticed people gathering and decided, on a whim, to join them.

Xavier was a Hungarian architect working in Ottawa. He'd stopped in London on his way to a UN course on architectural restoration. That's how he'd come to be on the walking tour that afternoon. As often happened with Xavier, he knew more than the tour guide; indeed, in the succeeding twenty-four hours he'd taught Wendy more about her own city than she had learned in a lifetime of living there. She had never dreamed there were magnificent sea captains' houses in the slums of the East End, or clay pits on the edge of Hampstead

Heath, or seven – or was it nine? – rivers running underground into the Thames. She worked out early on that Xavier was not particularly interested in women, which probably explained their easy friendship.

Although it was her first visit to Rome, Wendy found the Institute following Xavier's directions. And as promised, he was waiting for her in the third-floor cafeteria. 'Wendy, ma petite!' he shouted down as she approached. Looking up, she remembered what an odd looking creature he was. Jim described him as a gargoyle, all twisted up with secret vices. She thought he looked more like a pixie, with his sparkling green eyes and low-slung ears sticking out from his face.

'Ma petite,' Xavier hugged her, 'my little one; she has arrived.' The group around Xavier spread out to include her. 'This is blabla from Rajasthan. And blabla from Rio. And Curtis from New York . . .' Still stunned from her travels, Wendy couldn't take in any name except 'Curtis'. Xavier explained that he had to get back to classes and arranged to meet her again at six.

Wendy wandered around the district, then stopped in a bar and ordered a coffee. As she was sitting down with it the manager rushed round the counter shaking his finger angrily at her: 'You stand; you must stand.'

'Oh yes.' She remembered reading something in the guide book about having to pay extra to sit. She apologized and hurried out into the street.

A few minutes later she found a bench, but as she was easing onto it, a group of young men sidled towards her. She decided to go back to the Institute and wait in the cafeteria. She was exhausted; she and Jim had argued till three am. And she didn't care all that much about looking at architecture anyway.

At six o'clock Xavier appeared, surrounded by a group of people. She noticed, with a tinge of regret, that Curtis wasn't among them. Xavier asked about Jim and London, then glancing at the clock, he jumped: 'It's late; we'll have to run!' The group, which had been watching in silence, jumped in unison. The man from Cologne picked up Wendy's bag and they all rushed off behind Xavier.

Dodging through alleys, across crowded squares, down narrow streets, they drew to a sudden halt in front of a magnificent palazzo. Xavier approached a fruit seller packing the last of his oranges into a crate. A few seconds later he shook the man's hand and shot off round the back. Beside the car park he found a low entrance and led the way up a narrow staircase, then down a passage to a small door.

Putting his finger to his lips he turned the handle. They were at the back of a huge concert hall. As they slipped into the last row, Wendy noticed the ticket booth at the other end. 'It helps to speak the language,' she whispered.

'You're telling me.' Curtis twisted round; he was sitting right in front of them. 'The tickets cost twenty bucks each!'

'When did you get here?' Xavier hissed. 'I was worried about you.'

'Family problems,' Curtis shrugged.

'I told you before, Curt; you can run away from your problems, but they'll always catch you up.'

Before Wendy could discover what the problem was, the orchestra began tuning up. When Mozart gave way to Messiaen, she turned her attention to Curtis. He had a mischevious, sinister smile. He looks like a rodent, she thought; a rat, perhaps. No; he looks like Jack Nicholson.

When the concert ended Xavier hailed Curtis. 'You're coming back for supper,' he said. Curtis smiled and fell into line as Xavier led the way through the night streets.

Xavier's flat was in the Via del Diavolo, a windy passage off the flower market, described in Wendy's guide book as 'one of the city's most picturesque and least salubrious'. It smelled of garlic mingled with urine. As they turned into a courtyard Xavier pointed out a stone Madonna carved into the wall, lit up by a flickering candle. 'Every night the candle is there, every morning it's gone,' he explained. 'I've never seen anyone bring it though.'

The flat itself was cramped and dark. An odour of onions steamed past as they opened the front door into the hall. 'Heavens!' Curtis teased, 'you haven't actually cooked it yourself?'

'We do have a guest tonight,' Xavier grinned, 'and you've had a difficult week.'

'Now don't you start fussing about me,' Curtis chastised affectionately.

The table was already set with chipped bowls and mismatched glasses. Dinner consisted of overcooked spaghetti, followed by sheep's cheese and grainy coffee, interspersed with several bottles of red wine. Wendy didn't learn much during the meal, but she did gather that Curtis had a wife in a loft in Manhattan.

When the evening was over Xavier insisted that Wendy see Curtis off while he cleaned up.

'Tell me about him,' she said on her return.

'What's there to say?' he replied, sweeping the bread crumbs into his hand, spreading them along the windowsill. 'For the birds,' he chirped.

'You must know something?'

'He's the only other English-speaking person on the course.'

'What else?'

'What else do you need to know'

When the kitchen was spotless, Xavier pulled out the sofa and made up the bed. Before disappearing into his room, he explained that the following day he had to visit Hadrien's Villa; 'A stock exchange, and before that a warehouse, and before that a convent, and before that it was Hadrien's Villa in the Campo de Mars – the Fields of Mars – the battleground outside the town wall . . . But today it's just one of hundreds of restoration sites in the city.' Having no plans of her own, Wendy decided to tag along.

When they arrived the next morning a gaggle of people from the course was already waiting outside the gate. Curtis was not among them. Fifteen minutes passed. The group got restless;

several drifted off for coffee, several of those did not come back. Xavier disappeared and returned with the foreman. A few minutes later they were issued with construction helmets and ushered onto the site.

The building was encased in scaffolding, which in turn was wrapped in plastic, to keep the rain off the workers. Up three flights of ladders, round three corners they reassembled at the top of the villa. Below them young women in steel-toed boots worked with toothbrushes scraping centuries of grime from the honey-coloured stone. Above them, in the newly cleaned portal, the words 'Jonathan Jacobs, 1872', scratched with a penknife a century before, had been preserved through the restoration: 'It's part of the building's history – like the crosses the nuns carved over their headboards, or the counting marks the merchants made.'

This was explained by the foreman in Italian. The translator had had an accident; the one sent to replace her could only translate into French. 'Xavier speaks French,' someone shouted, so Xavier stepped forward to translate from the foreman's Italian through the translator's French into English.

'They're spraying the stone with ozone-free water . . . They'll cover the building with a layer of silicone . . . The project has taken eight years . . . In two decades they'll have to do it again . . .'

'What sort of water they use?' the architect from Rajasthan asked.

'Do they use ozone?' the stonemason from Cologne inquired.

'Please, what coating?' the art conservator from Peru requested.

'How long it all takes?' the urban planner from Seville wanted to know.

When the tour was finished Wendy took Xavier aside. 'None of them understand English, do they?'

'Nope,' he replied.

'So why did you bother?'

'Because I was asked to.'

'But what was the point if they don't understand? What's the point in the course at all?'

'The Institute is financed by America so the course has to be given in English. The participants are supposed to speak English; none of them do, but that's the convention.'

'So this whole thing's a complete waste of time!'

'Wendy darling,' Xavier patted her arm, 'do you suppose it's important for an urban planner from Mozambique to know how the Americans are restoring a Manhattan skyscraper? Do you suppose it's important for me to know how the Senegalese are preserving their huts from the coastal wind?'

'No, I don't suppose it is,' she said. 'So why are you here?'

'Because I'd be crazy to pass up six months in Rome looking at buildings.'

'But why did the government send you? Don't they realize . . .'

'Of course they do. And they also realize that I might meet an architect from Istanbul who's looking for a firm to design concrete modules or trucks to carry lumber through the jungle, and I might convince that architect to hire a Canadian company. It's all about communication, darling. It's not what's said; it's what's beneath it that counts.'

Curtis suddenly appeared. 'I'm going to the Porta Portese,' he said. 'Like to come along?'

Xavier shook his head. 'I've got to write up a site report. You go ahead though,' he added to Wendy, 'it's famous for Nazi paraphernalia.'

On the way Wendy learned that Curtis' problem was his wife: 'What other problems does one have – wives, husbands, lovers – unless you're like Xavier and travel alone? In which case you have no problems so you take on everyone else's.'

At the market Curtis bought Wendy a lace shift which he noticed her admiring. And Wendy bought Curtis a plastic bird that pecked frantically when it was wound up; she wanted to give him something and this seemed to amuse him. It reminded him of Barb, he said. Barb was his wife. He had asked her to join him but she had refused – till she lost her job last month, and the loft was burgled last week, and the car was smashed two days ago. And yesterday she had rung to say she was coming. 'She's done this to me before,' he muttered. 'We separated several years ago . . . but somehow that didn't work either and we just drifted back together.'

Curtis blushed, suddenly shy. He leaned on the hood of a car and pulled a pack of cards from his pocket. 'Ever had your cards read?' he asked. Wendy had not. He laid out the cards in an intricate pattern. 'Your present is dominated by a dark woman,' he said, pointing to the Queen of Spades.

'I don't know any dark women,' she mused.

'Wait and see. And here,' he pointed, 'a dark man; a good force.'

'I don't know any dark men either.' Curtis was the only dark man she knew . . . and she didn't really know him yet.

'Perhaps you don't know him yet,' Curtis replied. 'Journeys. You have a journey: the Six of Clubs – a short trip . . . perhaps this visit to Rome . . . and with it comes some revelation: the Nine of Diamonds – a secret revelation which will lead to a change in your circumstances. Anyway . . .' he swept up the pack, 'you can make of it what you will. I learned it from a guy in the army. A gypsy. At least, he said he was.'

'Is it accurate?' Wendy wasn't sure how seriously he took it all.

'Works for me,' he shrugged, shutting the cards away. 'I've gotta get on; I'm expecting a call. Can you find your way back to Xavier's?' He gave her vague instructions and strode off in the opposite direction. Suddenly he stopped: 'Hey!' he called back over his shoulder, 'have you been to Minerva's Temple? Check it out.' Then he disappeared.

When the sun goes down in Rome, it goes down quickly; Wendy noticed it was almost dark. Repeating Curtis' instructions over and over like a mantra she negotiated through the streets of people drawing down shutters, locking up doors. As the last light faded, she found herself in the flower market. Crossing the square, littered with dead leaves, she turned down the sinuous Via del Diavolo. The candle flickering by Madonna lit her way to the door.

That evening they went to an Italian dubbed American film about a fascist architect dying of cancer while his wife had an affair with a foreign diplomat. The audience whispered and giggled throughout. 'Germans,' Xavier pronounced as they jostled their way through the crowd at the end, 'language students; probably sent along to pick up the spellings.'

The next morning Wendy mentioned that she wanted to see Minerva's Temple. Xavier, who had a talk to prepare, arranged to bring her bag to the station later that afternoon. Despite his detailed map, she approached the Temple from the wrong side, across four lanes of weekend traffic. After veering round crazily honking cars, she passed through the ancient columns into the silence of the interior. Once inside she discovered that the classical façade masked a perfect Byzantine church; the Roman temple had been taken over by the Christians in the eleventh century – Minerva was lost in all but name.

As her eyes adjusted to the dark Wendy felt the place was alive. Fresco women gazed at her in almond-eyed serenity. Golden icons glittered near the ceiling, candles glowed beside each altar, the odour of incense and roses permeated everything. She sat for five, ten, fifteen minutes . . . then suddenly, feeling faint, she hurried out through a small back door.

Emerging from the silent chapel into the midday roar, she found herself in a crowd of Japanese, shrieking around a large stone carved with a lion's face. In the centre of the stone was a hole: 'La Bocca della Verita' – the Mouth of Truth. A sign on the wall explained that if you told a lie with your arm in its mouth, the creature, the Bocca, would bite off your arm. The tourists were testing the legend, jamming their limbs into the dark cavern amid squeals of laughter and truth and lies.

When the tourists moved on, Wendy approached the stone. The face was ancient, primitive, at once sinister and mischevious. Amazing, she thought, this pagan ritual being enacted on the site of a pantheistic temple, which had been converted to a Christian church, which still operated in this post-Christian, post-Freudian, post-nuclear age . . . It wasn't a very lucid thought, and it didn't mean much, except . . . except . . . She thought of time, of her life, and of Jim. And suddenly none of it seemed significant. Except that she had a plane to catch and was due to meet Xavier in forty minutes.

As she turned to go Wendy noticed a gypsy selling souvenirs. Behind the postcards were some resin models of the Bocca della Verita. The least expensive had a mouth so small it was almost closed; the next size up could just accommodate a child's finger. She bought the third size up – the mouth on this model was big enough to fit an adult's finger. Then she rushed off to the station.

Xavier was waiting at the bar. Curtis was with him. Curtis smiled.

'I've just come from your Temple,' she said.

'And?' he asked.

'Strange place.'

He winked at her. 'Did you see the Bocca?'

She nodded.

The airport bus was almost full. 'Take care,' Xavier shouted through the door.

Curtis followed her onto the bus. 'Don't worry about the cards,' he whispered, 'they always turn out for the best.' Then he kissed her forehead. A chaste kiss, but full of potential. 'I'll visit you in June on my way back to America,' he called, dashing down the aisle as the bus revved up. Xavier had already disappeared, but Curtis stood on the platform waiting till the bus pulled away.

Jim wasn't at Heathrow to meet her. There was a message: a meeting he couldn't avoid; he would come round that evening.

'I bought you a present,' Wendy announced, later, as they lingered over the wine. 'It's a Bocca della Verita – a Mouth of Truth. You put your finger in this hole; if you're lying, it bites it off. Let's try it.'

He giggled.

'Come on,' she took his index finger and inserted it into the hole. 'Do you love me?' she asked.

'Who else would I love?'

'Yes, that's a good question: who else do you love?'

'This is silly.' He tried to remove his finger.

'"Yes" or "No" answers only. Do you love somebody else?'

'Wendy, I'm getting tired of this.'

'Yes or no?' She held his finger.

'No. I told you. Now come on!'

'Why won't you move in here? Are you having an affair? With a dark woman perhaps?'

'Wendy, this isn't amusing.' He twisted, wrenched his finger free. 'Look, I have an early start tomorrow. I brought my bike over; I have to leave now.' To his surprise she put up no resistance.

A few metres down the road from her flat, Jim swerved to avoid a cat. His bike wobbled an instant, then toppled down on top of him. He sprained his wrist, pulled a tendon and – of course – he broke his index finger. When Curtis came to visit, Jim was living, unhappily, with his mistress of two years. Wendy, who didn't like living alone, welcomed Curtis handsomely.

Maps

I dreamed I was standing behind you. I wanted to clean the windows. They were streaked and greasy and clouded with dirt so you couldn't see through them, but I wondered, Is this part of my job? Would it be overstepping the mark? I was afraid you might get angry. I was afraid you might fire me if I cleaned the windows.

I dreamed I was walking through a desert with somebody, a stranger. It was a woman. She had long hair, pulled back in a French braid. She had my mother's face, but it wasn't her, my mother. A storm was coming; I could tell, though she didn't realize. The sand was swirling round us. We were sinking in at every step and I had to keep my eyes tight shut to stop the sand from blinding me. I wanted to get away from her – it was my mother now – but I knew I had to look after her, and I didn't know how I would manage with my eyes closed.

I dreamed I was stuck on a glacier. Alone. It was cold, so cold, and nowhere to hide. There was no shelter, no trees, just rocks and ice. I'd left my spade behind so I couldn't even dig a hole. I only had my red hunting hat. I thought I could cross the glacier. I thought there would be trails. There weren't. The first night my fingers and toes froze. The next day they burned. The day after that they turned brown, then green, then they all dropped off and slithered into a stream. They were snakes, with little faces where the toenails and fingernails had been. And as the current swept them away I suddenly realized that I hadn't been alone before, that they had been with me, my little companions. But now they were gone, and I really was alone. So I climbed into my sleeping bag and slid down the ice to join them. I couldn't swim, but that didn't matter, I would slither into the river and meet them somewhere further along. But the river had frozen, hard as a highway, blacker and blacker as night drew on. And for the first time I knew I was really going to die.

I dreamed I was a child again. I was arguing with my mother. 'But what if you're wrong?' I kept saying to her, 'but what if you're wrong?' She didn't reply.

I dreamed you'd come in with an armful of carrier bags from the shops. You were pleased with yourself, and I was delighted; I thought, Thank God, he's making an effort. But when I opened the bags, all they had was paper towels. Nothing else, just paper towels. And I said to myself, I mustn't be cross, I must encourage him. But I was so disappointed. We needed groceries: food and wine and lightbulbs and toothpaste, and all you got was paper towels.

I dreamed I was walking down a street with a group of old friends, school friends. You weren't there, it was before I knew you. Suddenly I was in the country, I was sailing in my boat, with my little brother. I was at the helm. He was sitting in the middle, taking the wrapping off packets of sandwiches. The sun was hot and the wind was good, and we were racing along. That was it. That was all. But I was so happy, I can't tell you.

I dreamed you were a baby. It was your face, it was you, but on a baby's body, a classic, naked, kicking baby's body. The odd thing was, you had a man's tie around your neck.

I dreamed my mother was pregnant with another child. Now. At her age. But I knew it was my brother she was carrying. It was as though he wasn't here yet, although even in the dream I knew who he was, I knew him as his adult self. I was furious at her – at my mother. I thought, What a stupid, stupid thing to do at your age. I thought, I'm not going to take care of you any more.

I dreamed all the fillings fell out of my teeth. My mouth was full of chalky white grit. I dipped my finger between my bottom lip and my gum and tried to scoop it out, but there was always more, more of the grit. I tried to spit it out, but there were little bits I couldn't get rid of.

I dreamed you had a baby.

I dreamed the cat came back. I was sitting in the garden and he just walked through the hedge and came and sat in my lap and I thought, Oh, it's Felix; so he wasn't dead after all. A few minutes later he got up and left, but before he went he winked at me. I think he had your face.

I dreamed I was the President of the United States. I was being sworn in. As I put my hand on my heart I was thinking, I wonder if I'll be assassinated? I wonder if I'll be able to do it, to do the job properly?

I dreamed there was smoke rising up from the street. I knew the tube was on fire. People were running everywhere, I could have stopped someone and asked, to be sure. But I felt, as long as I don't ask anyone, as long as I don't know for sure, then it might not really be on fire. Then a little girl came up behind me and put her hand in mind and walked along with me.

I dreamed I was in the mountains, trying to find a walking stick. But every time I found a good branch and cut it down, it turned into a snake in my hands; it suddenly went all limp and slid away.

I dreamed an estate agent telephoned and tried to sell me a two-bedroom flat. I recognized the man's voice; it was the voice of your business partner. I said: 'Mike, it's me.' He replied: 'I know who it is,' then kept on trying to sell me the place, so I realized it wasn't Mike, it really was an estate agent. But as he described the place I realized that it was your office that was up for sale. I kept trying to understand what that meant; whether you were going to move your office into the house. Or whether you were secretly selling the house as well. Or whether you were trying to get the estate agent to convince me to buy the flat so I would leave, so I would move out.

I dreamed I checked into a hotel. The floors were cold, the place looked like it was crumbling, but I had no choice, it was the only place around. They gave me this horrible little room with a horrible carpet, a purple carpet that smelled of cat piss. I was especially mad because I knew an actress down the hall and I knew that she had a beautiful room with huge windows and wooden floors. Bare floors, stripped and polished and shining like a mirror. And when I woke up in the morning there were two birds, a pigeon and a starling, flapping around me. I was trying to shoo them out, without letting the cat get at them. Suddenly I was covered in these birds which just wouldn't go away. 'Who owns this place?' I shouted. 'Trusthouse Forte,' someone shouted back. 'Well it's just not good enough,' I replied, 'it simply isn't good enough.'

I dreamed I was in a houseboat, in a room in the boat, it was a library, walls lined with books, ceiling to floor. The boat was moored beside a huge mansion, a grey shingled mansion. The boat was also made of shingle. And it was leaking. Water was seeping in at the seams. The books were getting mouldy and expanding with the damp. At first I tried to stop up the holes, but they kept springing open and the water kept leaking in and I was in tears, crying at you: 'It's leaking because you didn't help me make it. You knew how, but you wouldn't give me a hand!'

I dreamed I discovered you'd married my brother. Everyone knew; they all kept it a secret. We were all at a party when I finally realized, watching you together with him. I was furious. I became bitchy about it: 'Well of course,' I said to someone, 'she's such a snob, such a prude, it's a perfect match.'

Later you took me aside and said, trying to console me: 'When they write our biographies they'll say he was a substitute for you.'

'But it won't be true, will it,' I replied. You shrugged. 'There's no way we could make it work,' I continued, 'but it still hurts that you chose to marry him!'

I dreamed I was on a picnic with my mother and my sisters. I must have been about eight years old. It was a place we used to go to as children, a large flat rock at the top of a hill rolling down to the river that ran past the house. Mum was sitting on the rock with her knees up; I was sitting between her knees. We were both looking at a bird, a bird with bright blue feathers, in a tree which was quite far away.

I dreamed I was skiing; the black run on the highest slope in the Alps. I was alone. I was the only one on the mountain. There was a fresh snow; it had covered most of the rocks. It was magnificent.

I dreamed I was living with a dead body. A corpse. I knew it was a corpse, but somehow that didn't matter. Finally I decided, though, that I would have to do something about it, to get rid of it before it began to stink. I had to arrange the funeral. That's what scared me most; I didn't know how you do it, how you go about arranging the funeral, that's why I hadn't done it before. I don't remember what happened next except that it was a Gothic, cabaret sort of thing – the funeral. I suppose that means it was alright.

I dreamed I was out in the boat at night. I was lost, but I knew you could navigate by the stars. I looked up; there were masses of stars, and I didn't know how to steer by the stars anyway, but then the sky clouded over till there was only one star left, and I realized then that that was the star I should steer by.

I dreamed the princess and the prince married and they both lived happily ever after.

Bullshit

You want to know what happened to her after her divorce? She packed up the house in London, sold the paintings, gave the cats away and went back to Canada to live in a corn field with a twenty-three-year-old pig farmer she met one day on a train. He was half Irish, half Italian, he talked with an Ottawa Valley twang and ended his sentences with 'eeh'. They say you tend to return to your roots. She was a Taurus, her roots were always in manure.

Morning

The earlier train had crashed outside White Plains, killing a bunch of rich kids heading back to their schools in the States after the Christmas break. Twenty, forty . . . Casualty figures rustled around like a breeze which suddenly rises from nowhere. Jenny wished their mother hadn't insisted on seeing them off, now she knew about the crash too.

Lou returned from the ticket counter. 'The train could be delayed for hours, Mum,' she warned. 'You'd better get back on the road.' Although it was only just past noon, the sky had that swollen, menacing look of an impending storm.

'She seems to get smaller each year,' Jenny muttered as the Honda skidded away.

'It's just because you don't see her that often.'

'I didn't plan to live abroad, you know!' Jenny felt guilty. Every time there was a crisis, Lou, who was younger and poorer, had to give up her lessons and cover her shifts and hike up to Canada to sort it out.

'That's not what I meant,' Lou said quietly. Outside it was still; the icy stillness of dead cold. The room was fogging up with bodies. Two French nuns were chattering; everyone else sat in silence. Thinking about the crash; the casualties; twenty, forty, sixty dead.

A porter appeared. The room sprang to life: people zipping up cases, lacing up boots, hurrying out to the platform. Finally she heard it: the low moan, like a loon on a summer night. Then silence. People stopped stamping their feet to see if they'd simply imagined the noise. The nuns stood beside a mother and son. A row of hopeful faces, rooted on the platform. Like sunflowers, Jenny thought, following the sun across the sky. But these were frozen, staring down the track, at emptiness.

'It's coming,' Lou pointed. The hole where the track seemed to disappear was a dot; then a circle; then the nose of the train, transforming itself infinitesimally slowly. It was a trick of the climate, that the train sounded like it was moving away when really it was approaching.

The carriage was dark and smelled of cigars. It started to snow: fat flakes, smashing against the glass. 'Mum will be only half way home.'

'She'll be on the back roads by now,' Lou lied, 'it's the highway that's dangerous.'

If she skids on the ice, slides into the ditch on a country road, what then? Jenny thought. She can walk, in the dark, in the freezing cold, in the blinding storm, to the nearest farm. And what then? Jenny thought. They chunted on in silence. It was three o'clock. In two days I'll be home, Jenny thought. Home: London home, not Home: the farm. She hated going back. Going back to Canada. Going back to England. Going back always meant leaving somewhere.

Minutes? Hours later, the train slowed to an easy stop. The platform swarmed with lights. People loading things. Unloading. A porter announced that the dining car was open. Lou pulled out a Thermos. 'If we can hold out, I know a great Spanish place . . .' Tonight, their last night together, was dribbling away in this stale train, in this stark carriage, in this freezing night, waiting for the bodies to be cleared off the track somewhere down the line.

Lou handed her a mug of tea. She wanted to talk. The space between the seats was too big. The tea was too sweet. The train shuddered then shunted off. Jenny noticed cars creeping along icy roads. They passed a clock tower: 7 pm. Mum would be safely home by now. *Should* be. She shut her eyes and opened them. They were passing through another town: White Plains.

The town where the crash had been. She looked for wreckage along the track, relieved that it was too dark to see. She willed herself not to look at her watch: 9 pm.

She woke with a jerk. 'We're here,' Lou said.

'Shit,' Jenny muttered as they emerged; five past eleven; the evening's shot.'

'Nonsense,' Lou headed for the lockers. Everyone else scurried straight for the door. 'We'll store your things here,' Lou explained. 'You'll have to come through the station tomorrow to pick up the airport bus; it'll save us going back to the apartment now.'

'We can't go out tonight; you're working tomorrow. You'll be exhausted!'

Lou stuffed the key into Jenny's pocket.

A group of men jiggled restlessly, guarding the exit: 'Smack, Crack, Ecstasy . . .' Lou marched between them, brushing them off. From the echoing emptiness of the station they fell into Forty-Second Street. The neon scream of Forty-Second Street. The snow piled high at the sides of the road magnified every light like a prism. Jenny stopped to take it all in. She was suddenly warmed by a memory of that summer seven years before, the summer she'd spent in Manhattan, when every day was forty-eight hours and every hour was a lifetime.

'Women don't stop on Forty-Second Street. Especially at night.' Lou poked her as one of the men who was watching broke rank and advanced.

'Where are we going?'

Lou stepped into the street and whistled – two fingers, a screech: a taxi pulled over. 'Nathan's,' Lou instructed, as the driver whirled them into the traffic and down through a stream of yellow lights.

'I thought you had a Spanish place?'

'Later,' Lou promised, 'it's too early yet. That time I visited you in New York you took me to Nathan's, do you remember?' Jenny didn't. She must have been terribly broke

133

to take a newcomer to Nathan's, she thought, as they stepped out in front of the dreary façade.

Jenny sat in a booth. Across the steel counter, doubled in the mirror behind, four black teens in white uniforms dished thick plates of food to hollow-eyed customers. The place was huge. The people were tiny.

Lou returned: two hot dogs, piled with sour-smelling onions: 'Welcome to the Big Apple.'

Jenny tried not to think of udders and eyes, lips and anuses, all the things that go into hot dogs. 'What next?' she asked, wiping her mouth with a napkin from the dispenser chained to the table leg.

'A film,' Lou replied. Jenny looked puzzled. 'It ends on Wednesday and I'm working all week.'

'Right,' Jenny tried to get into the spirit. 'What's the film?'

'It's French Canadian actually. An art film.'

Jenny's spirits sank. 'Sounds heavy,' she said.

'It's a comedy.'

As they stepped back into the windy street Jenny prayed they wouldn't take the subway. Four months living in Manhattan and she'd never mastered the subways. She only knew one route – from the SoHo room she'd shared with her boyfriend, up to the editing job in Midtown. One subway line, two stops, then three blocks' walk. There had been a more direct route, but it would have required her to change trains.

Suddenly Lou waved. 'That's our bus!' Against all odds the driver stopped. The side door opened with a puff.

A man got on behind them: a tramp. 'I'm a poet,' he declared. 'You two sisters?' Lou nodded. 'I'm a poet,' he repeated. 'What's your name?'

'Louise,' Lou said.

'And hers, your snooty sister's?'

Jenny concentrated on the shops sliding by.

'That's Jenny,' Lou replied. 'She isn't snooty, she's looking out at the streets. She's from London,' she confided. The man fell silent, then raised his head:

'As I was going up the stair
I met a man who wasn't there.

134

He wasn't there again today
I wish to hell he'd stay away.'

Jenny recognized the verse from a book of children's rhymes.

'It's a kids' rhyme,' the man explained, 'with a slight variation of my own.'

Then he continued:

'Lou and Jen, two sisters fair,
Exploring the Manhattan night,
Chanced upon a troubadour,
Who dared to speak, and caused them fright.
Jen refused to sit and stare,
Demurely looked away,
Lou, less frightened, didn't care,
She was the more polite.'

Jenny looked at the man. He was younger than she'd thought. Perhaps he wasn't a tramp. Perhaps he was a writer.

'This is our stop,' Lou announced, standing up. They were on Bleeker Street. It was calmer here, the lights were constant, no throbbing or flashing, they simply illuminated the signs: Michael's Pub, The Cookery, The Blue Note, MacDougal's.

Lou headed into the Late Nite Fix. The film was half over. They tiptoed into the back row. It was a talky film. Young Urban Professionals ruminating on life and love and sex in a summer house. The characters, the conversations, even the accents were familiar.

Suddenly, with no conclusion except the end of a day, the film was over. The credits rolled. The audience stirred, gathered belongings, drifted away. Jenny stayed on, Lou beside her: Costumes, Hairdresser, Location Manager, Caterer, and Thanks to, and Copyright of, and finally the last credit: Translated by . . . Billy Black.

'Billy Black!' Lou nudged Jenny. 'Do you suppose it could be . . .?'

'Must be.'

'Is he still in Montreal?'

'Last time I heard. It was years ago . . . It must be him; I'm sure it's him. It's exactly what you'd expect him to be doing.'

Billy was a boyfriend from university. He'd been one of the Montreal mafia, the French cliques – writers and artists with their new-found *Vive Le Quebec Libre'*. He normally shunned English girls like Jenny; she never understood why he'd gone for her. A short relationship anyway; she had ended it. And since then, in New York or London, when recreating her past for some new lover she had wondered about Billy. Idly. As one wonders about people one once vaguely knew. And here he was . . . The music faded. The room went dark.

The foyer clock read one am. 'Where now?' Jenny asked, rushing to grab a taxi disgorging two men in drag.

'Sancho's.'

'The Spanish place?'

Lou nodded. 'Eighth Avenue and something – Sixteenth – I think,' she called to the driver. 'It's somewhere in the meat district.'

The taxi refused to go beyond Eighth and Fifteenth. 'It's just that he won't find a fare in the area. Nobody lives here; it's perfectly safe.'

'Great, we could scream till eternity and nobody would come.'

The streets were empty, lined with warehouses. A truck lumbered past, transporting carcasses. They turned a corner. Two people were huddled round a fire in the gutter. 'Hellllooooo,' the woman called. The word expanded between the buildings. 'Wanna stop and warm up?' the man offered.

'No, thanks,' Lou explained, 'we're going to Sancho's.'

They walked on. Their breaths, like dragons', swirling around them; like the exhaust from an idling engine, like the steam rising up from the holes in the road, the only other signs of life. We're lost, Jenny thought; are we lost? She didn't want to ask; she didn't want to make the possibility real by putting it into words.

Suddenly, a light glowed: Sancho's. The door opened into a dark, smoky bar. A couple of men were in the corner, heads together, muttering low. Behind the counter a squat woman with a dark moustache called out to Lou. 'Darling,' she cooed, 'you're back! Two margaritas?' Lou nodded.

'In this cold?'

'It'll warm you up.'

The woman produced two glasses of thin, green liquid. Lou swallowed hers back in one gulp. 'Hey, Sancho,' she called. 'Where's the phone?'

'It's almost 2 am you know,' Jenny warned, as Lou dialled.

'Jack? It's me. At Sancho's. Great. A friend,' she explained, replacing the phone, 'another painter. He lives up the street.'

They'd downed two more drinks by the time a blast of cold air announced Jack's arrival. He was tall, blond. 'Let me guess,' he grinned, 'you're the sister. Come on,' he said, 'Jojo's running the club.' Jenny hated to leave the warmth.

Jack put his arm round Lou who put her arm round Jenny. They walked in a line along the road. Trucks rumbled past. The fire still burned. 'Hey, Jacky, you struck lucky tonight,' the man shouted, poking the flames with a stick. 'C'm'ere, Jacky boy,' the woman motioned. 'Got any cash to spare? There's a dear.' He pulled a couple of bills from his pocket. They fluttered slowly in the cold, grabbed in a cackle of glee.

They walked till a low pulse vibrated the air. There really is a club, Jenny thought. She was too cold to be dreaming. Jack banged at a door. It slid open. 'Jack!'

'Jojo!'

Jojo was black, with scars, like whiskers, across his face. He wrapped the three of them into one huge, crushing, embrace. 'This is my sister,' Lou shouted. Jojo stepped back and shook Jenny's hand, then he slid her onto the dance floor: 'Any friend of Loulou's is a friend of Jojo's too.'

It was too crowded to really move. Just as well, Jenny thought; she hated dancing; she never seemed to find the

137

rhythm. She concentrated. There was no rhythm. Looking around at the bodies beside her she realized they had no rhythm either. It was just noise. Just pulse. Just beat. Track melded into track, you just adjusted your gyrations to the new beat.

Two bottles of beer and a daiquiri later Jenny yawned.

'Time to go home,' Lou decided.

'You go,' Jojo pouted, 'let her stay.'

'She's got a plane to catch.'

Jack was dancing with a brunette, so Jojo led them through the dance floor. He kissed Jenny, a lingering kiss, then shut the door behind them.

'You know he's gay?' Lou mentioned, wrapping her scarf round her head.

'Of course,' Jenny chuckled. 'Who? Jojo or Jack?'

'Both,' Lou shrieked, 'though neither one knows it.' They burst into laughter.

'Oh God,' Jenny gasped, trying to pull herself straight, 'we'll never get a taxi at this hour.'

'We can walk from here.' Propping each other up, they set out.

'It must be late.'

'Early,' Lou countered, and they dissolved into giggles again.

'Oh no!' Jenny suddenly snapped. Paused. 'Hick! Oh no; oh please no. Hick!' She juddered.

'Oh Christ, not your hiccoughs!'

'Hick!'

'I'll get some water.'

'No, no wait! Hick!'

'I'll get Jack, he can drive us home.'

'Don't leave me here! Hick!' She giggled. 'Hick!' She jerked with the pain.

'I won't be a minute.' Before Jenny could stop her, Lou darted off.

Jenny's hiccoughs were notorious. One bout had lasted eight hours, and only stopped in the taxi on the way to the hospital. 'Hick!'

She leaned against the building behind her. Giggling, hiccoughing, gasping for breath. She could feel the bricks scraping her back. 'Hick!' She slid down the wall. Beside her a grill in the sidewalk was steaming: heat from the subway below.

'Hick!'

Sometimes she could cure her hiccoughs by lying down.

'Hick!' She lay on the pavement, over the grate.

'Hick!'

The sky was turning from black to grey. Tomorrow? Today? Soon she would be home. England: home. Colin would meet her at the airport. Mum would be home by now, on the farm. Sleeping with the cats lined up on her bed and the car safely locked away in the barn.

'Hick!' And here she was, in Manhattan, in the meat district . . . 'Hick!'. . . In the middle of the night. She giggled.

'Hick!'

Jenny woke to a sound of squabbling.

'Leave 'er be!'

'She's dead!'

'She isn't'

'Check 'er pockets.'

'Check 'er pulse.'

'She's sleepin', poor girlie; leave 'er be.'

She opened her eyes. The sky had pink streaks, stretching, spreading through the grey. Her view was almost obscured by a face. A woman, smelling of urine; a woman was standing above her. 'What'd I tell you, you've woke the poor girlie.' A bony claw snatched back from her side; 'Sorry, missus,' a man mumbled, 'thought you was dead.' He backed away.

Suddenly the sound of footsteps: Lou loomed above her. 'What's happening?' Jack was there. And Jojo with a jug of water.

'We didn't do nothin'!' the old man cried. 'We was watchin' over her till you come back.'

139

Jojo helped her to her feet. The air was cold against her back. She choked on the water that Lou was pouring down her throat. She turned to the tramps but they'd disappeared. The sky was more pink now than grey. 'The hiccoughing's over. It's alright, I've cured it.' It's morning already, she thought, looking around. It's morning already, she marvelled, when did the night disappear?

Sunday
Soaps

After Margaret had made the bed, and put Benny's socks and pants in the hamper, and wiped the toast crumbs from the counter, and dusted the rubber plant, and masturbated on the sofa, she was faced with the problem of what to do with the rest of the day. It was a problem she faced several times a week, but seldom on Sundays. Usually Benny was there on Sunday, but today he'd decided to visit his mother. As he had last Sunday and the Sunday before. He'd said his mother was poorly. He'd asked if Margaret wanted to come, but she didn't like his mother – to be more precise, it was his mother who didn't like Margaret. And so she was faced with Sunday alone.

Monday was a good day because Tippy came to clean. Tippy always had stories to tell, and between making Tippy's coffee and lunch and tea, and running out for rubbish bags or laundry soap, Margaret could be sure Monday would be busy. But then there was the rest of the week. A good week was one which had something to do every day – getting the car serviced, taking the bird to the vet, waiting for the electricity man. Good weeks were rare. Average weeks had two or three days with something to do. Bad weeks had only Monday filled. This was shaping up to be a bad week.

Margaret pulled herself together, got off the sofa, smoothing the cushions behind her, and went to the kitchen to make another cup of coffee. It was only her second cup of the morning, and though Benny said they should cut back she decided to treat herself to real coffee instead of the Tesco's instant which she kept for Benny's breakfast. Benny didn't like coffee anyway. It was one of those ironies which kept Margaret amused when she felt the black dog coming over her. She liked coffee: Benny didn't. She liked reading: Benny was dyslexic. She liked people: Benny preferred television. And yet it was Benny who got to sit in that bustling office reading reports with an endless supply of government coffee percolating just down the hall.

'Well, God; another wasted day,' she thought as she watched the bold, black liquid drip. It was only when Benny Junior moved out that Margaret began to think about God. Over the past few years she had concluded that He must exist. How else to explain how perfectly, and completely, and consistently wrong her whole life had been? Clearly there was an overall plan and she and Benny had simply got switched – put, by mistake, in each other's place.

Surely, she thought as she folded the bag of coffee and placed it behind the row of jars on the cupboard shelf, surely there must be hundreds of women who think, like Benny, that sex after forty is rude; that only factory workers holiday in Spain; that women should feel privileged to be taken care of; that the Connelly girls ought to shut their windows if they're going to play their music on summer nights. He was an easy man to take care of. He was relatively neat. He never drank or swore at her. He worked hard every day until eight and every Saturday he spent at the clubhouse – no women allowed – so she had all the time in the world to herself. And some women, she thought as she took her coffee back to the lounge, some women would give anything to have such a man.

But she – with the perversity which she concluded was proof of a Devil to match the non-infallible God – she, Margaret, was discontent. She would almost rather he hit her. Or at least forced himself on her occasionally. And she certainly wouldn't mind if, like Mr Johnson next door, he brought his friends home. The problem was he had no friends. They had no friends. Benny didn't like her speaking to the neighbours, he said they were common. He also insisted that she hire Tippy to clean once a week even though they couldn't afford a cleaner and certainly didn't need one.

Although she didn't talk to them, Margaret often listened to the Johnsons arguing through the walls:

'Whaddya mean there isn't enough? I work all day to pay for the food, all you have to do is put it on the table; if there isn't enough, go and get more.'

'You haven't been working you've been drinking, you're stinking of the stuff, the lot of you; Kenny and Gary don't even have work and Roger should go home to his own table once in a while instead of sponging off us all the time.'

Then Margaret would hear a slam as Mrs Johnson stormed out of the house down to the shop on the corner. But by the time Mrs Johnson came back up the street with her bags of potatoes and tins of baked beans she would be humming and he would be glued to the match and Margaret would envy them both.

Margaret also happened to know – because she often heard them in the dark when she couldn't sleep – that although the Johnsons were older they still made love. Indeed they made quite a racket when they made love. Margaret couldn't imagine what they did to make so much noise. She also couldn't understand how Benny could sleep through the noise. But he always did. Out like a light; slept like a log. Winter, summer, spring and autumn.

By now Margaret's coffee was cold. She wanted to masturbate again. She tried to limit herself to once a day but this was, after all, a Sunday, so she might just allow herself one more go. Though you had to be careful, she reminded herself. Between noon and two was a dangerous time; that was when the travelling salesmen came by, expecting to find 'the lady of the house' preparing Sunday dinner.

I'll see what time it is, she thought. If it's past noon I won't do it. She got up and went round to look at the clock. She kept it behind the door so she'd have to get off the sofa occasionally. It was ten minutes to twelve. She took her cup back to the kitchen, washed out the filter and buried the paper in the rubbish bin. Just in case Benny should notice.

Not that he was likely to be in the kitchen, Margaret thought, but there was no point in displaying the fact that she treated herself occasionally.

When she returned to the lounge it was noon. Too late to masturbate, so she turned on the television. It was the soap opera from Australia. The woman with the crippled daughter's husband was having an affair and everybody knew but her – the past two episodes the woman had kept almost finding out; but then finding other explanations for the evidence. Margaret found the series particularly irritating because the woman was unbelievably stupid about her husband's affair. But she watched it because there wasn't anything else to do, the library was closed on a Sunday and she'd already finished her book for the week.

A few minutes later the telephone rang. The person on the other end hung up without speaking. That's funny, Margaret thought, the same thing happened last Sunday too; and the Sunday before. She'd meant to mention it to Benny, but somehow it had slipped her mind. I wonder why he keeps on ringing.' She knew it was a 'he' because the breath on the line was too deep for a woman.

She shrugged and turned back to the programme. The woman was making Sunday dinner. Her parents were visiting, because her husband was away on business – at least that's what he'd told her; but everybody else knew he was off with his mistress. The woman was just taking the roast out of the oven when her telephone rang. You knew something disastrous was coming because the music got faster:

A man's voice said, 'Emma?' (Emma was the mistress' name.)

The woman answered: 'This is Judy Smith.'

The man hung up. The woman shook her head and began basting her roast. Then the phone rang again and music raced again. It was the man again. He said, 'Edward Smith. I want to speak to Edward Smith.'

'He isn't here,' the woman replied. 'He's away on business.'

'He's away on my business,' the man's voice was trembling, 'he's gone off with my wife Emma.'

146

The woman shook her head, bewildered. 'No,' she said to no one in particular, since she was alone. 'No. That's not possible!' Then the telephone receiver fell from her shoulder, banging her arm, making her drop the pan of hot grease all down her tweed skirt, her slender, stockinged legs, her gleaming kitchen tiles. But she didn't seem to notice.

Margaret switched off the programme and sat on the sofa staring at the blank TV screen. No, she thought, there isn't a God. There isn't an order. There isn't even a pattern in which I have been misplaced by mistake. It is all random. Some people have good lives. And some people have lousy lives . . . and I am simply one of those.

The
Wild
Flowers
of Crete

'You going into town?'

Tay shook herself; the scruffy young woman was speaking to her.

'You wanna share a cab?'

'Oh. Ah, yes, I suppose.' Tay looked around: 'I was going to share with that woman . . . Francis, Fran . . . The American over there . . . I'm sure she won't mind a third person though. What's your name?'

'Leigh.'

'I'm Tay. Sorry, I don't function too well this time of the morning.'

'The cheap flights always come in at this hour. I just checked with the Cosmos guide; he said not to pay more than six hundred dracs to get into town. How many pounds is six hundred drachmas?'

The city glowed a dirty neon in the pre-dawn chill. Several men stood, smoking, round the taxi stand. *'Pensione?'* Tay ventured – Italian was the only foreign language she could speak. One of the men disengaged himself and ambled over to a dented Mercedes. The girls threw their luggage into the back and stumbled in on top of it. He drove them to a dingy hotel where Tay recognized two women from the London flight coming down the steps. 'No rooms?' she asked.

'Too expensive,' they replied. It was four in the morning.

151

The concierge wrote a price on a notepad.

'Four thousand,' Fran said, 'how much is that?'

Tay calculated, 'About sixteen quid.'

'I've only got eight hundred dollars to get me to Asia,' Fran's eyes were brimming with tears of fatigue. 'You go ahead; I'll wander around till it's light.'

'We might as well stick together.' Having sat beside this bleary-eyed foreigner all the way from London, Tay felt responsible for her. 'Are you sure it's too much?' she persisted, catching the driver's exasperation. 'We might not do any better.'

'It's less than six quid each,' Leigh added.

'What's a quid?' Fran asked.

'A pound.'

'A pound? A quid is a pound?' Fran paused. 'Oh, for six pounds I can do it.'

A few minutes later Tay lay in her bed. An arm's length away Fran, stripped to her knickers, was removing her contact lenses; her thighs had that orange-peel texture that only comes with age. When they'd first spoken in the queue at Heathrow, Tay wondered how old Fran could be. She hesitated to ask, afraid that Fran might be younger than she.

'Do you suppose it's possible to call Saudi Arabia from here?' Fran asked, climbing into her bed.

'It's closer from here than from London.'

Leigh emerged from the bathroom. 'You know, girls,' – she pronounced it 'gels'; Leigh worked in the Dorothy Perkins in Watford and hated it – 'you know, girls, this is the most luxurious hotel I've ever stayed in, that I've paid for myself. I mean, *en suite* bathroom and breakfast included; it's as good as the Holiday Inn any day!' She perched on the corner of her bed and unwrapped a small, brown, cellophaned package.

'Is that dope?' Tay asked.

'Mmm. Do you smoke?'

Tay shook her head. 'But most of my friends do,' she added hastily.

Leigh took a piece of tissue and began wiping down the cellophane. 'I was on holiday here years ago; couldn't find the stuff anywhere.'

'Isn't is dangerous bringing it in?'

'Yeah,' Leigh grinned, 'if you're caught they beat you up and who knows what . . .'

Tay wanted to ask how she'd smuggled it in:

– Did you hide it on your person?

– Did you carry it up your bum?

She decided to abandon the question.

'Sure you won't share a joint?'

'Thanks, no,' Tay smiled, 'but you go ahead . . .'

'Na,' Leigh muttered, rewrapping the dope, 'it's no fun on your own. As she slipped into sleep Tay wondered if she should have left her purse on the chair, or whether, like Fran, she should have tucked it under her pillow.

At ten the next morning the concierge woke them with a sharp knock: 'Breakfast finish in five minutes,' he called through the door.

Leigh groaned, then jumped up. 'I paid for it, I'm eating it.'

As they lingered over tepid Nescafé, Tay pulled her Blue Guide from her purse, relieved to find its contents undisturbed from the night before.

'You been here before?' Leigh asked.

Tay shook her head. 'It was the cheapest flight I could get, on a few hours' notice.' She flipped back the cover of her guide book to see what country she was in. Cyprus? Corfu? She knew it began with a 'C'. Ah yes, she remembered: Crete. The travel agent had sent her to Crete. That was less than twenty-four hours ago . . .

'So, what're you running from?' Leigh persisted.

Tay had vowed not to discuss it. 'A rotten marriage, actually.'

Leigh turned to Fran. 'And you?'

'Me?' Fran looked half asleep. 'I'm travelling around the world. In six weeks,' she added, as though to forestall any more questions.

'What are you looking for?'

'Time to think.'

'About what?' Leigh wouldn't be put off.

'About a relationship with a schmuck,' Fran confessed.

'Well me, I'm running away from a ratbag,' Leigh announced. 'I'm going to find a beach and bake myself brown and beautiful so he regrets what he gave up. The scum.'

Tay turned a page. She hadn't been alone in years. Twenty-four hours ago the prospect of a week on her own had seemed bliss, but already she was dreading it.

'Well,' Leigh spoke, breaking the silence, 'I'm going to hitch. A man on the plane recommended a place: Paleohora – cheap, no tourists, on the south-west edge of the island.'

'I read about it,' Fran said, 'I thought I'd hitch there myself.'

Tay suddenly recalled the thrill of putting oneself at the whim of fate – the prospect of a chance encounter which could turn into a meal, or a drink, or a bed for the night, or perhaps a sticky situation, or perhaps nothing: an afternoon in the baking sun or the pouring rain, standing by the empty road. 'I'd like to hitch too!' she exclaimed. 'Shall we all go together?'

Leigh looked doubtful. 'Three could be a drag.'

'I don't fancy hitching alone though.'

'I'll go alone,' Fran volunteered, 'I've never had any trouble.'

'No,' Tay insisted, 'you two go; I'll take the bus.'

'Oh fuckit,' Leigh exclaimed, 'we'll try it; what have we got to lose?'

They decided to test their luck at a large intersection on the edge of the city. Leigh went first; in her leather jacket and tight jeans she seemed the most likely to secure a ride. She stuck out her thumb while the other two sat on the luggage, looking inconspicuous. After ten minutes Tay took over. She eyed the passing drivers like a fisherman luring and teasing his prey. After a quarter of an hour Tay conceded to Fran. With her bulky sweater and wrinkled sundress Fran looked the least promising. Three minutes later a van pulled over.

Leigh jumped into the cab. The drivers, two boys, gestured for one more up front. Tay was determined it wouldn't be her. She wanted to think. Waiting by the side of the road, her mind had drifted back to the problem at hand. Which was to say the situation with Bill. The Affair. 'I must think about The Affair,' she thought, but try as she might, she couldn't think what to think. She couldn't imagine Bill with another woman. She couldn't imagine The Other Woman. She couldn't think why Bill had done it, or how he thought she would respond. She lay in the back of the van thinking: I must think about this.

Meanwhile the boys were trying to impress them by parroting pop songs. Leigh giggled appreciatively. Fran ignored them and pulled out her map.

'Damn!' she said, a few minutes later.

'Problem?' Stellios asked, proud of his command of the language.

'We're on the wrong road.' The road they wanted was twenty kilometres west of the one they were travelling on. Stellios explained the situation to Georges.

'My friend, he is mad,' Stellios proclaimed a few minutes later. 'He say, you pay petrol, he drive you to coast. Fifteen hundred drachmas.'

'Sounds good to me,' Leigh chimed in. 'It's got to be cheaper than the bus.'

'Get him to take us to Ayia Galini,' Fran pointed to a seaside town. The boys conferred again, then agreed.

'Ayia Galini very beautiful,' Stellios cooed, collecting five hundred drachmas from each of them. Georges whirled the van round and hurtled down a dirt road.

'Whoah up,' Fran looked around warily. 'I don't remember this.' They drove down a twisted street and slammed to a halt beside a small house with three scrawny goats tethered to the front gate.

'One minute,' Stellios hopped out of the van. Fifteen minutes later he returned with an armful of cassettes.

'Great,' Leigh squealed, 'tunes for the road.'

'Great,' Fran echoed, wearily; Tay nodded sympathetically. Soon they were rattling down the narrow highway, wrapped in American remixes of out of date English pop songs.

'How extraordinary it is,' Tay thought, gazing out of the window as Crete unrolled behind her, 'you make a decision and somehow, almost inevitably, it happens. There you are, in Crete or Cyprus or Kathmandu, with a bunch of strangers with whom you've thrown in your lot for an hour or a day or a week. And life goes on. And Bill has no idea where I am.'

He'd know by now that she'd gone. He'd assume she'd gone to her parents', but he wouldn't risk ringing, just in case – he wouldn't want to have to explain why he was calling if she wasn't there. So he would be mildly worried, and extremely annoyed. But whatever he was thinking, Tay thought, he'd never think that she was here, in the hot sun of an early spring, banging around in the back of a van, looking at poppies and wild irises and white lilies – single, sullen stocks standing alone on the edge of the road. She'd never seen lilies growing before. She'd never seen lilies at all except in paintings of the Annunciation: with the dove or the word or the angel whispering in Mary's demure little ear . . . Whisper whisper whisper, secrets secretsecret.

'Daisies. Yellow Daisies.' She brought herself back to the flowers. 'Daisies. And those purple things that look like miniature hyacinths. And the olive trees. And the grape vines pruned to stubs, but in two months they will be flourishing. The thingness of things,' she said to herself, fighting off the tears. 'Immerse yourself in the thingness of things. The colours: purple, yellow, white. The smells – what smells? – diesel from the engine. And sweat. And the vague lollypop scent of orange trees. Yes, the orange trees, with both flowers and fruit on the same tree; who'd have thought that one tree could mature at such different rates . . .' But it was too late. The tears overcame her. She wiped them away as she stared resolutely through the back window. 'Things; things; colours; smells,' she thought, 'rock, dust, clay – dotted with these indomitable wild flowers. This riot, this chaos, this carnival of flowers. Even Solomon in all his glory was not arrayed . . .' And still the tears flowed.

A few minutes later Stellios insisted on sitting in the back. Tay, still stretched across the luggage, examined the boy. He couldn't be more than sixteen, she mused. He looked down at her, oblivious to the tear stains streaking her cheeks. 'How old are you?' he challenged.

'How old do I look?'

'Twenty? Twenty-two?'

'Thirty.'

'No,' he said. 'Not possible.'

'Thirty?' Leigh shouted from the front. 'You're joking! You're not thirty.'

'I'm thirty-one,' Fran muttered.

'Jesus,' Leigh shook her head. 'How do you two do it? When I get to be that old I'll be all haggard . . .'

'How old are you?' Stellios turned to Leigh in a suddenly seductive tone.

'Twenty-three, mate, and it's older than you.'

'How old you think me?'

'Twenty,' said Fran.

'Eighteen,' said Leigh.

'Sixteen,' said Tay, annoyed at his arrogance.

'Wrong!' he declared. 'Seventeen!' He drew the figure on Tay's shoulder.

Her first instinct was to withdraw her arm. 'Oh hell,' she thought, 'if he wants to flirt with a middle-aged wreck . . . In fact . . .' her wicked id mused . . . 'his face is so smooth, his flesh is so soft . . . Forget it!' her alter ego advised: 'He's probably a virgin; he wouldn't know what to do with it anyway . . .'

Tay allowed herself to be flirted with, until a sharp turn threw the boy on top of her. 'Shit!' she muttered.

'You blossoming?' Stellios grinned.

'I'm blossoming?'

'Yeah, you blossom: "Shit". You blossom. You teach me some English blossom?'

'Oh blasphemy!'

'Yes,' Stellios sighed, exasperated. 'You blossom "Shit".'

'Sure, I blossom shit.' Tay replied. 'I'll teach you to blossom.'

157

'Dirta bat.' Stellios pronounced, delighted.

'Dirty bastard – that's right.'

'You dirta bat,' he repeated in a heavy American accent.

'He must have learned it from television,' Tay thought, as he snuggled up beside her.

'Dirta bat,' he muttered low, his face beside her ear.

Tay replied in a whisper: 'Shitface. Fuckhead. Scumbag. You dirty bastard. You two-timing, deceitful, lying, coward-ly . . . shithead.'

'Slow!' Stellios said. 'Say slower.' And swatting some imaginary thing, his hand brushed her arm and came to rest against her breast.

'Heavens, this is real kids' stuff,' Tay thought, suddenly recalling the six months it had taken Bill to make love to her. At the time she'd assumed he was shy. Later she'd decided that he simply didn't care for sex, a conclusion which was challenged by her recent discovery. 'Maybe it was just sex with me that he didn't care for . . .' Before she could stop herself the tears were dribbling down her face. Stellios horrified, withdrew his arm and sat bolt upright, banging his head on the roof of the van. Fran turned round to see Tay in tears and Stellios looking bewildered.

'Time to switch places,' she announced, climbing into the back, taking the guide book from Tay's purse. 'Thirty-five K's; it shouldn't be long.'

An hour later they rolled down a steep hill into the village of Ayia Galini:

'I think we made a mistake here,' Fran muttered. Every house was newly whitewashed. Every house had a 'Rooms to Let' sign. Every house had a ground floor bar called Zorba's. As they rounded a corner, the sea spread out before them. It was translucent, fluorescent; it was blue like the newly-painted front doors; it was blue like a postcard, a painting, a poster.

'Oh my God! Look at that water!' Tay cried.

'We go to beach.' Stellios winked at Georges.

'Go to the bus station,' Leigh insisted. 'I want to get out of this place; it looks like a film set.'

At the station they found that the bus from the city would have cost half the fee the boys had extorted for petrol, and the next bus to Paleohora didn't leave until dawn the next morning.

'Now we swim!' Stellios sang.

'Let's split,' Leigh muttered. 'If we have to spend the night in this town I don't fancy spending it with them.'

'Oh,' Fran raised her eyebrows. 'I didn't think you . . .'

'Yeah, well I do.'

'I'm with you,' Tay announced, hauling her bag from the back of the van. A bar nearby was playing The Beatles' 'Norwegian Wood'. 'Who'd have thought,' she mused, trying once again to fight back the tears, 'who'd have thought when he wrote the song, two decades ago, that it would be playing in an off-season island, to a trio of women escaping their lovers.'

The boys, bewildered at the sudden mutiny, shot out of the village in a squeal of tyres. 'Thank God they're gone,' Leigh flounced down the street and flopped onto a bench facing out to the sea. Tay and Fran followed, dragging their bags. In the harbour a wire clinked against a flagpole. Scraps of dialogue drifted across the square. Tay re-ran all the conversations of the past few months trying to work out when it had begun. The letter that fell from his pocket gave no clue. Several kisses. No date. No name. No indication of whether Bill had made the rendezvous . . .

And who had seen them? Who knew about it – which of her friends? Who had conspired with Bill to arrange the places they could meet, to arrange to see her alone so Bill could have the night with his lover? 'Christ!' she thought, 'how could he, how could he, how could he do it to me!' She wanted to find a place to hide. To cry. She wanted to find a place to lie down. She wanted to crawl into a hole and never emerge.

She pulled herself up. 'I'm going to look for a place for the night.' Leigh and Fran followed. An old woman watched them walk up from the harbour.

'Rooms?' she asked, leading them to a stairway between two tavernas. At the top of the stairs she unlocked a door: the room had a double bed and a balcony overlooking the street: 'One thousand drachmas.'

'But it only sleeps two.'

'That's alright,' Fran said, 'I'm sleeping on the beach.'

'Don't be silly,' Tay replied, 'we can fit three in here.'

'No, really, I'd rather.'

'Is it the money?' Tay rapidly calculated her cash. 'I'm sure I could . . .'

'No. Honestly. I prefer it.'

'I'd join you,' Leigh looked annoyed at Fran's independence, 'I'd join you, but my sleeping bag's not that good.'

Fran followed the old woman out of the room. 'Must stake out my place before dark; I'll meet you back here for dinner.'

When they'd gone Leigh stretched out on the bed. 'You don't mind sharing, do you?' she asked, and promptly fell asleep.

Tay sat on the terrace and tried to concentrate. She'd refused to give up her passport, preferring instead to pay in advance. She'd been careful not to use traveller's cheques which could be traced. She'd stressed to the travel agent not to tell anybody where she had gone. She was determined that Bill wouldn't find her here. Wherever *here* was. Cyprus? Capri? It began with a 'C'. She searched her bag for the guide book. It wasn't there. Fran had it last. Shit. Where was it? Had she left it behind? Where the hell was she? Tay thought of Bill, of travelling with Bill. He always knew where they were. He always knew the significant things about each city. He always was irritated by her lack of geography; he said she simply didn't care enough, or she'd remember things. Like where she was now.

She'd been lost before. They'd been travelling in Spain; she'd gone for a walk. She didn't speak Spanish, she didn't know the name of the village so she couldn't ask for help. She was walking and walking, along a dusty road, and the sun was going down when he had driven up behind her in their little red car. He was furious and worried sick. But when she burst into tears he'd held her, and they'd sat by the side of the road, somewhere in Spain, while the sun went down, and he'd held her and rocked her and told her he loved her, and she'd wept and finally she'd fallen asleep, and he'd driven her back home to bed.

She remembered another time in Italy. And another time in London after a fight; she'd stormed out in a fury and hidden behind a wall in the park. And he had found her. Two hours later. 'Two hours,' she had thought at the time, 'two hours isn't bad in such a large city, in such a large park.' They had gone home, laughing about the fight, which, like most fights, had been about nothing.

And as she thought about the past she found herself thinking: 'If he finds me, if he finds me here, in this place, in this country I don't know, in this village whose name I've forgotten, if he cares enough to find me here where nobody knows I am, if he finds me I will go back to him.' And even as she thought it, she knew that it would be wrong. 'He lied. He betrayed you. He did it once, he will do it again. Affairs are addictive.' She knew that – from her own parents, from her married friends – once you start you can't give them up. She knew he wouldn't, now that he had tasted the thrill of illicit liaisons. And still, in some corner of her mind, she was holding on to the thought: 'But if . . . but if he manages to find me . . .'

It was dark when Fran returned from the beach. 'Where's my guide book?' Tay asked, not meaning to sound so abrupt.

At the sound of their voices, Leigh woke with a start. 'What time is it? I'm starved.'

'It's eight thirty and your book's in my pocket.' Fran handed it to Tay. CRETE was emblazoned across the top. Of course: Crete. Off the south coast of Greece. How would she remember it? Crete, rhymes with cheat. Bill was a creep to cheat on her. She wouldn't forget it again.

'Did anyone notice a phone?' Fran asked as they sat in the empty taverna.

Leigh perked up, sensing a story: 'Who is this Saudi person, anyway?'

'A friend.'

'Not the rotten relationship?'

Fran shook her head.

'Still . . . Saudi's a long way from Oregon . . .'

'You're telling me,' Fran sighed. 'He's a loner. Give him a desert island, he'd be happy as a pig in mud. That's the problem, of course . . .'

'I see.' Leigh filled Fran's glass. 'Men are shits.'

They sat in silence while an old Cat Stevens song wafted through the cacophony of Green/French/English pop music: 'Oh, baby baby it's a wild world, it's hard to get by just upon a smile . . .'

'He's blown my whole world away,' Tay thought. 'We had a good life and he's destroyed it. How can I believe in anything; my friends . . . my judgement . . . my own life . . .'

'Well, girls,' Leigh emptied the bottle and motioned for another, 'I can't sit here any longer without confessing. I know I'm a shit, but I don't feel guilty. The man I'm running away from is a married man. He's just in it for the sex; that's all I'm in it for too. His wife's out there cooking the dinner, waiting for him to come home and he's with me in the Holiday Inn ordering Chicken Supreme from room service. Finally I thought, What kind of shit is this; he'll never leave the kids, so what am I wasting my life for? I told him it was finished. He didn't believe me. I mean, life's boring enough, why give up a night at the Holiday Inn with room service and a jacuzzi. But I had to do it. So I walked into the travel agent on Tuesday morning and Tuesday night I was on the plane, instead of in that room with brown bedspread and the all-night films. And you know – I really don't miss it that much. Not as much as I thought I would.'

Fran looked into her glass; 'My guy back in Oregon, he could have been your man.'

'How does he do it? How do they get away with it!' Tay cried.

'For him it was easy: two nights a week I'm on call at the clinic. Two nights he's free to do as he pleases.'

'I'd leave him,' Leigh pronounced, the wine beginning to sound in her voice, 'I'd leave the fucker; no man of mine's going to screw other women.'

'I'm almost thirty-two. I want to have kids.'

'How did you find out?' Tay asked.

'I rang once too often in the middle of the night. He confessed, he apologized, he swore it was the first and last time. Then I heard from a friend about another woman. An earlier one. Who knows how many there were before. You know what he said: he said he couldn't promise anything. He wants us to live together but he won't promise not to see other women.'

'So what did you do?'

'Changed my shift; took a pay cut; lost my seniority. But I'm home every night.'

'You're not home tonight,' Tay muttered.

'Tonight I'm thinking,' Fran replied.

'I wouldn't put up with it!' Leigh declared, after a few minutes' silence.

'If they do it once, they'll do it again; that's what I can't bear,' Tay sighed.

'You're right there, girl,' Leigh drained her glass. 'I'm here to tell you. He slept with me the day my girlfriend ditched him. I didn't know it at the time. He's our boss, see. I'll bet he's at the cashier now. Doesn't waste his time, him. Hey, what are you looking at! Look, she's gone white!'

Tay was staring at a man, 'That's my . . .' He turned around; she slumped.

'He's not going to come for you, girl,' Leigh scowled. 'You said he'd never find you in a million years. You said you'd spit in his face if he came round the corner, so what do you want?'

Fran called for the bill.

'I'll walk you back to the beach,' Tay said. 'I want to make a phone call.'

'You're not going to ring him?' Leigh spat in disgust.

'I'm going to ring my parents to see if he's been looking for me.'

'Leave him. Forget him. That's my advice.'

'You haven't been married for nearly a decade.'

'So what are you doing here? Why not fly home right now and tell him you're sorry you broke up his game?'

Tay shrugged.

Leigh shrugged, 'I'm going to bed. Any preference which side you sleep on?' Tay couldn't remember which side she slept on. She slept with Bill's arms around her. Always. Even during the affair. Right up to the last night they'd slept together. And who were his arms round tonight?

'Are you ringing your fellow in Oregon?' Tay asked as they wandered down to the harbour.

'No, this guy in Saudi; my closest friend. He said he might meet me here in Crete. I haven't managed to get through to him yet.'

They found the phone kiosk near the sea. Tay rang first. She got a crossed line: a man was yelling, a woman cajoling. When she finally got through to England, there was no reply. When Fran got through to Saudi a woman answered the phone. Her friend wasn't there. He'd be back next week. The call cost her four thousand drachmas: sixteen quid: thirty-two American bucks. 'And I've only got eight hundred dollars to last the next three weeks,' she moaned.

'You're sure you'll be alright on the beach?' Tay asked.

'Sure. Fine. See you at the bus,' Fran smiled. She looked like a little girl with her huge back pack and her wrinkled sundress. Tay wanted to kiss her. Instead she headed up the hill.

Tay woke to see Leigh, naked, brushing her long, blond hair. 'What a beautiful body,' she thought. 'That sleek stomach, those thighs; bodies like that only come with youth.' She pretended to sleep.

164

'Hey,' Leigh croaked, shaking the bed, 'hey, we've got a bus to catch. It's a quarter to six!'

Tay jumped out of bed. 'What if Fran doesn't show up?'

'That's her problem,' Leigh shrugged. 'Who'd 'uv thought it . . . with her little sundress, who'd 'uv thought she'd sleep on the beach. Just goes to show,' Leigh muttered, spitting on her contact lenses.

'Goes to show what?'

'You can never tell with people. You can never really know 'em. However much you think you do, there's always room for surprise.'

'You're telling me,' Tay thought. 'The one thing I knew – absolutely – was that Bill would never be unfaithful. What an archaic word: unfaithful. Breaking faith. Well, he certainly broke mine . . .'

Leigh threw a shoe at her: 'Step on it, girl; it's five minutes to six.'

They arrived at the station just as the bus came flickering down through the rising mist. Fran was waiting outside the station. 'I was afraid you two softies had slept in.'

'No chance,' Leigh grinned. 'So, where're we headed?'

'I think the first stop starts with an "H".' Tay pulled out her guide book. 'Hania, or Chania, or Xhania.' It was spelled differently in each of the travel agent's pamphlets. Eventually she found it – spelled 'Khania': a port city; second in size to Heraklion; remnants of Venetian . . . noted for the bravery of its citizens under German occupation . . . Not worth staying in, Tay decided; she'd push on to Paleohora.

The bus hummed along the narrow roads scalloping the mountain. The landscape of the interior was not as barren as the land by the sea; rocky ridges held patches of extraordinary green, and on the most implausible precipices tiny vineyards grew. Pushing up through the olive nets were poppies: tart little red proclamations shining against the grey crochet. Tay loved poppies.

'I love poppies,' Leigh announced as though reading her thoughts. 'Whenever I see poppies I know it's going to be alright . . . There's a place in Morocco,' she continued, speaking more to herself than to Tay, 'a little village called Tarazoute. I lived there all one summer . . . They have this tea made of poppies . . . You drink it with a slice of orange to take away the taste. Rashasha, it's called – Rashasha. It makes everything magic . . .'

An hour later the bus pulled into the Khania. Tay hated getting out; she was deep in a conversation with Bill.

– Can't you see, it can never work now.

– We had an enchanted life which you ruined . . .

–I'm sorry, Billy, we really had something special; I thought you understood . . .

He would plead and cajole and apologize. And slowly he would realize that this was the end. That he had destroyed the best thing that ever happened to him. And he would beg and cry, and she would remain firm. Because she knew it could never work now, however much they both wanted it to. And somewhere beyond fantasy she knew that Billy would only really respect her if she left him. That was the irony of it all.

As they scouted round the station Fran noticed a telephone. 'Shall I ring him?'

'He's away,' Tay replied.

'Oh, yes. I forgot.'

'What do you want from him anyway?'

'I'm going to ask him to marry me.'

'Whoa, hey!' Leigh proclaimed, 'That's the spirit, girl!'

'What if he says no?' Tay asked.

'Then I'll go back to Oregon and get pregnant.'

'I see,' said Tay.

'You're mad,' Leigh sighed, 'there are other fish in the sea, you know.'

'Who wants to marry a fish?' Fran replied, her face impassive as a plate. Leigh and Tay collapsed with the giggles while Fran stared, sadly, at the floor.

There was an hour's wait for the bus to the coast. Leigh watched the luggage while the others went to buy fruit. Down a dirt street between two apartment buildings they found a woman selling oranges: one hundred drachmas, forty pence, eighty cents, for three oranges the size of grapefruits. 'Sweet. Very sweet. Very good,' the woman assured them. She was right; they were sweet. Like honey. Like nectar.

The bus to Paleohora was crowded. Leigh gave up her seat to an old man and sat out the journey in Tay's lap. Paleohora was an ugly town. Modern. Industrial. The main street full of tavernas; a few narrow side roads led down to the beach. 'Another mistake,' Tay thought, but she'd decided, whatever happened, she would stay there for the rest of the week. She wanted to think, to sleep, to sit in the sun and think about nothing; you could do that anywhere.

As they tumbled out of the bus a herd of old men hobbled forward: 'Rooms. Zimmer. Pensione?' Leigh and Fran headed towards the water, planning to sleep on the beach. Tay followed an old man through a gate, to an onion-domed church; in the churchyard a swing hung from a tree. They went through the fence, down a camomile path. The smell reminded Tay of the hot, dusty days of her childhood: those endless afternoons with nothing to do. She had been an only child. She hated being bored more than anything. At least with Billy she had never been bored.

'But surely that's not enough,' she thought, 'surely I deserve more.' She stumbled and grabbed at a crumbling wall. The path led up a rocky incline; primitive steps were cut in the dirt. The man led her round a corner, up the steps to a house, with blue shutters. Three small rooms opened onto the terrace. An old woman appeared and unlocked a door: a narrow bed, a hook on the wall and a window looking out to the sea. 'I'll take it,' Tay said.

'One thousand drachmas,' the old woman replied.

'Five hundred.'

'Seven fifty.'

'Five hundred. I stay for five days.'

The old woman held out her hand. Tay counted out twenty-five hundred drachmas. The woman bowed, retreated. Tay dropped onto the bed. Through the open window she could see the turquoise blue of the water, the lighter blue of the sky, the grey-blue of the mountains, fading in layers back to eternity. She slept, and woke up ravenous.

It was dusk when Tay sat down at the bar by the harbour. She was served by a beautiful woman with long grey hair. The woman was English: she had lived in the village for seven years; she hadn't been back to London, she hadn't even been to the other end of the island. A little girl with long dark plaits crept up behind her whispering, 'Mama, mama,' into her skirt.

Returning to her room Tay found a little cup filled with wild flowers. The old woman must have put it there. The night was freezing. Twice she had to get up and put on more clothes. 'I'll never sleep,' she thought. At dawn she woke up, numb. She slept again and woke into a bright, clear morning. The sun through the window was warming her feet.

She ran into Leigh having breakfast in the English woman's bar. Fran had gone off. 'Funny little thing, isn't she . . . Independent as hell.'

That evening Leigh moved in with an Arab boy she met on the beach. He had been there three months, picking tomatoes. He was planning to return soon to his village in Morocco.

Tay spent her days walking on the beach, reading in her guide book of the sites she had no desire to see. She spoke, occasionally, to the English woman, and occasionally to the Arab workers who lived in dormitories, sending their meagre pay cheques home, and occasionally to the German boys who hitched into town, slumming it for a few days before moving on to brighter places. But mostly she just kept to herself. She was learning to enjoy solitude.

On her last evening Tay strolled down to the church. It had always been locked, but she pushed at the heavy door one more time. It opened slowly. A flame burned in a bowl of sand. Beside it was a box of candles. She took one out, and holding it against the flame, she said to herself: 'This is for Billy, I hope he will be happy.' She stuck the lighted candle into the sand and took another one from the box. Holding it against Billy's flame she said out loud: 'And this one is for me.'

Billet
Doux

It's one of those axioms that are so clichéd you forget that they're true, like, 'After long illness death is relief,' and, 'Sex the first time is disappointing,' and, 'Giving birth feels like dying,'; 'The cuckolded partner is always the last one to know . . .'

– My God, you mean you didn't know!

– How could you not know?

– Everyone knows! You must have known! I thought you knew! . . . And so it goes. And so it went for her.

She walked along the pavement, scouring the road. You can never find it when you're looking for it. She checked in the gutter, beside street lamps, telephone poles. She hurried to a patch of grass beside the intersection, surely this would yield . . . Nothing. Damn. She would have to try the park. She hadn't thought it would take so much time. She'd ordered the courier to be there in an hour. She would have to hurry.

Walking down the steep incline she noticed some in a garden. It was too small. Hard. It wouldn't do. She fingered the plastic bag in her pocket. She hoped it didn't have any holes. The traffic seemed especially busy. She stood on the curb; the park was beyond. A car turned slowly up the road making a gap in the traffic. She hurried across, over the smooth pavement, the stony verge, onto the soft, spongy grass.

She'd never been to the park on a weekday. There were more people than she'd have thought: mothers mostly, women pushing babies in prams. And kids. Couples. Too young to be unemployed; they must be skiving from school. She walked by the pond, up the hill, away from the people.

173

All those times she'd stepped in it, found it in her front path, smeared across her sidewalk, blotting up her garden; now she was looking for it there was none in sight. She found little bits: too small, or too dry, or too grainy. It had to be dark, to reflect the gold.

The place was full of people but nobody walking a dog. Finally she found some – a perfect patch: thick, rich, dark. But a few feet away two children were playing. She couldn't take it with them watching. She waited. They showed no signs of moving, so she walked on. Half an hour till the courier came. She noticed a dog running loose and ran after it. It disappeared. She walked on. Then she saw it: a large patch. It was older than she would have liked, and not as dark, but it was there. And nobody was watching. And time was running out.

She pulled the plastic bag from her pocket, slipped it over her hand like a mitt. She swooped down and scooped up a handful. It was soft. Doux. An image of her sixth grade French teacher came into her mind: 'Mamzel' – pert, petite. Blond. She slid the bag over her hand and wrapped it into a package, careful that nothing slipped out. It stunk. She hadn't thought it would stink. She hadn't thought about the smell.

Walking back past the children she wondered if they could smell it too. As she hurried through the park's front gates she saw a St Bernard. It was squatting up against a tree. Straining. Grunting. Steaming piles. She felt sick. She had enough already. She hurried home, the package stinking in her pocket.

She spread a newspaper over the table, pulled out her package, unwrapped it. She dumped it on the newsprint; some of it stuck to the plastic bag. It oozed out over the absorbent paper, creating a liquid halo. She unfolded the wedding paper – expensive paper: shiny, not absorbent. She scooped a spoonful from the newsprint and slopped it onto the wedding paper. Spread it thin, she thought, to fit into the envelope. Five minutes till the courier came. She pulled at the wedding ring on her finger. It stuck on the knuckle. She wrenched it. It gave. She slid the gold ring from her finger, placed it on top of the thin, brown slab. It shone.